QUEERLY LOVING

Edited by G Benson and Astrid Ohletz

#1

Table Of Contents

Miss Me With That Gay Shit (Please Don't)

Sacha Lamb

The worst thing that ever happened to me was when Nick Green went to Israel for that Teen Tzaddik thing and came back with a tan and no acne and I realized he was hot. But Elijah, you might say, what's so bad about that? Nick Green is kind of a dumbass, it's true. No one is going to deny that. But he's totally harmless. Why not just let him be his dumb, tanned, good-looking self and move on with your life?

The thing is, everyone always said Nick and I looked alike when we were kids. People thought we were siblings. But then puberty hit, and he got tall and I just got boobs, and Nick's acne was my sole consolation. Like, if he's getting the testosterone I want, at least he's not enjoying it. But it turns out all he needed to do was get food poisoning and almost throw up at the Kotel and I guess God feels sorry for him and he gets to come home with his skin as clear as the Mediterranean sky, and where does that leave me?

That leaves me with no consolation at all, because now Nick is the one with the hormones *and* he's the cute one, and that's not fair. It isn't fair at all. And also, he's still an idiot.

The first time I met new, hot Nick was at a Gay-Straight Alliance meeting, because God hates me as much as he feels sorry for Nick, I guess. It went like this:

"Hi, I'm Elijah—"

Nick, confused: "Eliza?"

"Elijah! Like the prophet? Jesus Christ, Nick."

"Wait, do I know you?"

As if we hadn't been in the same class at both real school and Hebrew school for our entire lives. Maybe he'd actually been replaced by a new, hotter clone, and the mad scientists forgot to give him back all of his memories. I mean, okay, so my twin sister got me a binder for our birthday and I'd finally convinced our dad to let me buzz my hair, and the family curse finally forced me to get glasses, but come on. I was still the same person.

"Oh my God, Nick, I was at your bar mitzvah! You were at *my*—mitzvah. Thing. Your mom gave my dad parenting lessons when he decided he wanted kids? I've worn your *hand-me-downs*."

Nick sort of leaned over and squinted at me. "Were you, like, always a dude, or?"

"Oh my God, Nick!" said Becky, who'd been out longer than anybody and considered herself the moderator for all discussions. "Not to go all Mean Girls on you but seriously, you can't just—"

Nick snapped his fingers, sitting up straight. "Wait, were you Aviva? Stern?"

"No, that's my sister."

"Sorry, dude. I used to think your sister was so hot."

After that, I pretty much missed the rest of the meeting. I was too busy trying to think of ways I could defeat Nick and steal his body for my own, leaving his dumb ass stranded in the fourth dimension.

The next time I saw Nick was at Rosh Hashanah. We both chose the same moment to try and slip out of service unobtrusively, and he literally smacked into me in front of the gender-neutral bathroom.

"I think the lock is broken," he said. "Want me to keep watch for you?"

I frowned at him. He beamed at me with all the innocence of a golden retriever. He had a couple of freckles I'd never noticed before. Last I looked in a mirror, I'd had bruises under my eyes like somebody had punched me. Nick was practically glowing. Who had authorized that?

"I don't mean literally watch you," he said. "That would be incredibly disgusting. I mean stand here and make sure nobody opens the door."

"No thanks, weirdo," I said. "You're missing the dvar Torah."

He rolled his eyes. "As if he doesn't give the same one every single year since forever."

"Please let me pee in solitude, Nicholas."

He gave me a sloppy kind of salute and started off down the hall, but then he stopped. "Hey, Elijah? Sorry about that thing I said. You know, at school? You look a lot different. And stuff."

He didn't stick around to explain what he meant by "stuff". Which meant I couldn't tell him he looked different, too. Which was good, because I didn't want him thinking it was a compliment.

"Hey, did you see Nick Green?" Aviva said, when I slipped back into my seat. "I thought he was you for a second. You wish, am I right?"

The thing about Aviva is that she always says the things I'm thinking that would be okay if I said them, but since she's not me, it comes across kind of tactless. I love my sister, but also, she is terrible.

"I hate Nick Green," I said. "He, like, forgot who I was."

"That's 'cause you got hot over the summer," said Aviva, flipping her hair over her shoulder and propping one heel on the edge of her seat. "No offense."

The other thing about Aviva is that she only says "no offense" after she's given you a compliment. I don't even know.

3

"Children," said our father. "Please wait until the singing to conduct your gossip. I am trying to fill out my Rabbi Kaganov bingo card and you are distracting me."

Nick found me on Facebook later, and sent me a friend request. His profile picture showed him standing in the sun somewhere, grinning at the camera. I ignored the request until he found me at school and asked if I'd seen it.

"No," I said. "I don't use the Internet."

That was a lie. I don't know why I said that.

"Good job, weirdo," he said, and gave me an encouraging clap on the shoulder like some kind of gym coach. Nick is on the soccer team, because of course he is. He looks great in shorts. I hate his calf muscles. At that moment, with him standing right next to me, my attempt to avoid his overly sincere eyes landed my gaze right on his stomach. I mean, abs. I was sorely tempted to punch him and see if they were as solid as I suspected. Maybe I would have, even, except somebody he actually knew yelled his name and he abandoned me in the hallway.

I friended him back later, and then I had to look at his grinning face on my news feed, like, every single day of my life. He had a million photos of himself. And also a million photos of cats, for some reason. I was ninety percent certain that Nick was allergic to cats, but that didn't seem to stop him.

As far as I could tell, he'd never been in a relationship with anybody on Facebook. I couldn't even find any photos of him with anybody that looked couple-y. What was he doing at our GSA meetings? He'd never explained himself and a good half the group were self-described allies who were there as much for Becky's cupcakes as anything, which meant I couldn't just assume Nick wasn't straight. It annoyed me without end that Facebook didn't seem to have any more answers than real life.

When I posted a photo of my cat, Nick liked it after about three seconds. *Wow Eli I didn't know you had a wrinkly alien in ur house :)*

As if he knew literally anything about me. He didn't even know that no one had ever called me Eli in my life. I had to close the tab.

TransProphet said: *tfw this dude youve known forever is like totally #transitiongoals but also he's totally an idiot & u r gay & filled with rage*

ViViStar reblogged this post and added: *lmao*

God, I couldn't even find a moment's peace on Tumblr. Isn't the Internet supposed to be a sanctuary? Why had I let my sister follow my blog? As if it wasn't enough that we had to share a uterus, presumably. Dad says he got us from a secret government laboratory, but that's obviously a lie. Although some days I could believe Aviva was specifically engineered to get on my nerves.

Things hadn't improved on Facebook in the two seconds I was away. Nick had posted a string of dancing cat stickers below his comment, leaving me with twelve identical photos of his face in my notifications.

Elijah Stern says: *its not a house its an apartment*

Nick GreenLantern says: *lol*

Elijah Stern says: *im not joking*

Aviva came into our room sometime after midnight. I'd been listening to her and Dad yelling at the TV for what felt like hours. My beloved parent and his only daughter get very worked up over sports. Maybe *that's* what he had her genetically engineered for.

"What have you been up to, nerd goblin?" she said. "You're sitting like a gargoyle again, by the way."

I dropped my feet to the floor and slapped my laptop shut on the desk. "None of your business, is what. Did we win?"

"You and Nick Green been sexting?" she said with her head in the closet, digging for pajamas. She came up with one of my shirts and put it on anyway. I didn't bother to object. You have to pick your battles with Aviva. "Did he tell you your weird cowlicks are cute?"

I didn't dignify that with a response, either. I just got up and got in the shower before she had a chance to brush her teeth. I needed time to think, anyway. Who has three hundred photos of himself on Facebook but never says a single serious word about anybody he may be interested in?

There was a logical conclusion, but I didn't want to believe it. I sat down on the floor of the bathtub and covered my face with my hands, despairing. What do you call somebody who either makes awkward jokes or says nothing? Closeted, is what.

Not only was Nick Green now attractive, it was very possible that he was gay or otherwise into boys. And I was still short, and squishy, and hairless. The true wrinkly alien of apartment 5B. If Nick was gay, it was the new worst thing that had ever happened to me. It was like my personal punishment from God, who apparently hated me so much he had to bypass nice honest Jewish smiting and go for that sneaky shit they loved in Ancient Greece. Maybe I should have tried harder to be sorry about stuff for the holidays.

I stayed like that until Aviva smacked the bathroom door, hard, and shouted, "Are you dead?!"

I should be so lucky.

The day after Yom Kippur, we got a paired assignment in history class. I was still in a low-calorie stupor and didn't even think about my abysmal field of partnership options until Nick dropped his notebook on the desk in front of me and announced, "Homework is anti-Semitic."

He said it loudly enough that everyone heard him and there was a kind of awkward silence. You could tell from her face that Mrs. Richards was trying to figure out if she should tell him off or ask for clarification or something. I guess she decided not, because she just said, "So, does everyone have a partner?"

And Nick grinned at me.

"What is this," I said, "a high-school drama?"

"What?" Nick asked. "Are you ready to kick some dead white guy ass?"

"Nothing. And aren't your grades, like, terrible?"

He just laughed, like he thought I was joking. I was not joking. I had read his entire Facebook going back to middle school, and I had it straight from the horse's boyishly handsome mouth. He complained about his grades all the time. Almost as much as I complained about mine. And now I had to rely on him to help me learn something? We might as well just lie down and die.

When I told him so, he looked confused. "Wait, I thought you were, like, super smart?"

"No, dumbass." I rolled my eyes so hard I could see the inside of my own cranium. It figured he wanted me to pull his weight. "That's my sister. Aviva. The one with the hair, and the breasts."

"Listen, when we were all mitzving it up, neither of you had any breasts," he said.

His tone of authority made me certain he'd looked for them and been disappointed. This was going to be the longest homework assignment of my life.

"So," he said. "Can I have your number?"

7

"Ooh," said Aviva, plucking my phone out of my hands. "Elijah's texting a *boy*."

"Shut up! We have a homework assignment. And I found a bra in the laundry that's way too small to be yours, you got anything to confess?"

"We did not make out on your bed," Aviva said. "So no. I don't."

"Children," said our father, without turning around from the collection of bubbling substances he had on the stove. "I am trying to preserve the image I have of you both as prelapsarian innocents, and you are making it very difficult for me with this conversation."

I snatched my phone back from Aviva and went to text Nick from the balcony instead.

Not that texting was exactly productive.

Nick Cheesy Grin: *yeah so I rly want a hairless one but my mom says they're creepy which is like*
Elijah Star Emoji: *slander*
Nick Cheesy Grin: *slander*
Nick Cheesy Grin: *lol jinx*
Nick Cheesy Grin: *but yeah anyway. sad lol*
Elijah Star Emoji: *she's not even weird once u get used 2 her like furry cats look weird 2 me now almost*
Elijah Star Emoji: *i mean i cd live w/o the kitty titties but u kno*
Nick Cheesy Grin: *lmao*
Nick Cheesy Grin: *itty bitty kitty titties, say that ten times fast*
Elijah Star Emoji: *pfff*
Nick Cheesy Grin: *so what was the assignment again*
Elijah Star Emoji: *u think i got a clue*

★ ★ ★

The thing is, it was very difficult to focus on homework when all I wanted to learn about was Nick's cryptic orientation. Sometimes,

I'd be convinced that he was flirting with me, and then he'd say something about girls and my soul would shrivel up and leave my body. He never really said anything conclusive. Sometimes he'd make jokes about bi people and I couldn't tell if he was making a confession or just behaving like kind of a douchebag. Maybe I was barking up the wrong tree entirely and he was aromantic. If so, he could have at least done me the courtesy of wearing grey-and-purple socks or something. There were so many possible ways that my crush on him could have been doomed from the start. I just couldn't figure him out.

The thing about Nick is, he can't commit to being serious for two seconds, except when it's schoolwork and other stuff that doesn't matter. Anytime I'd ask him about his personal life, I'd get some nonsense answer with a *lol* tacked on the end. I even tried being rude to him to see what would happen, but he just told me he liked my sense of humor. What the heck does *that* mean? What was I supposed to do with that?

Elijah Star Emoji: *so did u get up 2 teen hijinx in the land of our fathers*
Elijah Star Emoji: *Shari Goldberg says u threw up on the kotel*
Nick Cheesy Grin: *lmao not literally*
Nick Cheesy Grin: *I made a hummus related mistake & had to stay in the HOtel and miss the KOtel*
Nick Cheesy Grin: *finger gunzzz*
Elijah Star Emoji: *I hate you*
Nick Cheesy Grin: *lol u luuuuv me*
Nick Cheesy Grin: *but nah I didn't get pregnant or anything lmao*
Nick Cheesy Grin: *shit sorry is that offensive?*
Elijah Star Emoji: *I mean kinda but tbh ur entire existence offends me*
Nick Cheesy Grin: *sorry bro I'll try harder next time*

9

We got a B minus. I guess Nick wasn't as dumb as I'd thought he was. Turns out he complains about his grades because he's some kind of ludicrous high achiever. I couldn't believe it. What the heck was he doing with me as a study partner, then? He'd basically shot himself in the foot. He could have changed partners any time, and instead he kept texting me facts about Abraham Lincoln, and we got a B minus. He was the B, I was the minus. For some reason, this terrible decision on his part irritated me almost as much as the perfect not-quite-symmetry of his face.

Elijah Star Emoji: *why'd u pick me 4 a partner anyway dude*
Nick Cheesy Grin: *idk no reason*
Elijah Star Emoji: *u thought I was smart right. the ol lean on ur partner trick. sry 2 disappoint*
Nick Cheesy Grin: *no*
Elijah Star Emoji: *oh so u think I'm stupid...... I c how it is*
Nick Cheesy Grin: *omg dude no*
Nick Cheesy Grin: *I didn't mean it like that!!*
Nick Cheesy Grin: *I just thought we shld catch up and stuff :)*
Nick Cheesy Grin: *kinda an apology for how I forgot u exist lol*

"I'm gay, Aviva."
"I'm aware."
"I'm really, really gay."
"Yes, I know."
"He's such an idiot. Why am I like this? I'm dying."
"Please go to sleep, Elijah."

Nick Cheesy Grin: *anyway ur funny :)*
Nick Cheesy Grin: *anytime u need some1 2 teach u a thing*

Nick Cheesy Grin: *u know where 2 find me ;)*

I was pretty sure I was never going to sleep again.

"So Elijah," Aviva said. Dad was at shul, and we were eating challah French toast stuffed with jam and cream cheese. My sister sounded awfully businesslike for a girl who was holding one sticky hand in the air and typing on her phone with the other. "You're coming to Steve's party with us, right?"

"Who?"

"Steve Anderson? There's a party? Tonight? Ayesha and I are going? I need you to be our bodyguard?"

She says that every time, even though it is patently absurd. Aviva and I have the exact same amount of muscle mass, and Ayesha is on the soccer team and could lift both of us.

"I am not going," I said. "I'm tired of third-wheeling the Jewish-Muslim lesbian solidarity banquet."

"So ask Nick if he's going to be there, you can have some bro time."

"I'm not asking Nick Green on a fucking date, Aviva. What if he likes girls? What if he likes girls and he says *yes?* Anyway, who says I'm even interested?"

She gave me a sly look. "Who said anything about a date? You said it, not me. I didn't say anything about a date. I said bro time. For bros."

I pulled the hood of my sweatshirt over my head and laid my face flat on the table.

Elijah Star Emoji: *so u gonna b at Steve Anderson party later or what? my sisters breasts will b there apparently*

Nick Cheesy Grin: *lol Eli that's kinda sexist*
Nick Cheesy Grin: *but yeh*
Nick Cheesy Grin: *ur pex gonna be there? ;) lol*
Elijah Star Emoji: *wtf*

"What's up with you?" Aviva said. She'd been breezing in and out of our room in various stages of dressed up for about an hour. "I swear to God you haven't moved in ninety minutes. Are you coming with me tonight or what?"

"Nick sent me another wink emoji," I said. "The entire universe has been canceled. I'll never be able to look another human in the face again."

"Jeez, Elijah, why do you have to be so dramatic all the time? Put on a clean shirt, I *need* you to scare the boys away from me. I mean, look at me, I look amazing. Please, Eli-Eli, you're the only man I trust in this cruel world."

She did look kind of amazing. Maybe I could find Nick at the party and force him to explain himself. I dragged myself off the bed and went to steal the car keys before she could claim them.

Stealing the car keys was a mistake. Aviva seized the opportunity to sit in back with Ayesha and engage in a bunch of pre-party PDA, which consisted of holding hands and whispering a lot, which is almost as bad as making out to make you feel excluded. I love my sister, and I love her girlfriend, but also, they are terrible. Not that I ever say so in front of Ayesha. I've seen the look on her face when she has dinner at our house. She can't always tell when we're being affectionate with each other.

Anyway, if I had to be irritated at somebody, I was planning for it to be Nick. Two winky faces. Two. It had to mean *something,* right?

But on the other hand, he used to think Aviva was hot. And maybe the comment about my pecs was underhanded somehow. My pecs are one hundred percent artificial. He had to know that. Was he making fun of me? Maybe it was some kind of roundabout way of telling me to back off. Oh God, what if he thought I was hitting on him? I mean, I was, but what if he wanted me to stop? I was tired of wondering. Him and his stupid emojis. And his stupid face. And his stupid 3.8 GPA. By the time we got to Steve Anderson's house, I was ready to punch Nick, and his emojis, and even his GPA, right in the face.

Of course, when I got out of the car, all worked up, and Ayesha and Aviva ditched me to go dance, Nick was nowhere to be found. He had said *yes,* hadn't he? He was supposed to be here. We were late, because a Stern is never early. The place was packed. Better attendance than a test day at school, honestly. Steve Anderson has a pool and a brother who's over twenty-one, which makes his parties very exciting, if you're into that.

I'm not into it, and I was getting less into it by the second. I'd never realized before how many dudes with brown curly hair go to my school. The whole house seemed stuffed to the gills with Nick Green clones, and the man himself was nowhere to be found.

Elijah Star Emoji: *i said wtf*
Elijah Star Emoji: *& iiii say it again*
Elijah Star Emoji: *yo*
Elijah Star Emoji: *are you dead??????*
No fucking response.

By 11:45 I was feeling distinctly stood up. Dad said we should be home at midnight, which meant Aviva would be aiming for 12:30,

but I already felt like a total pumpkin. What was I thinking? Every decision I have ever made in my life has been terrible.

Getting drunk seemed like the appropriate ill-advised teenaged response, under the circumstances, but when I poured some vodka into my Coke, a single swig was so vile I was forced to reconsider. Adding more Coke didn't really help. How did people manage to enjoy this? I felt like the world's most pathetic mad scientist. My drink tasted like it was ready to start burbling and hissing and giving off smoke at any moment. I remembered someone told me once that it gets less nasty once you've drunk some, but it didn't seem to be working.

That's when Nick decided to show up, finally.

"Hey, Elijah? Can we talk?" He looked worried. He was holding his phone, which meant that it had not fallen down a storm drain, which meant that he had been ignoring me on purpose.

He looked like a dude who was ready to tell me that I was creepy and weird and needed to leave him alone. God, why did I ever let Aviva talk me into stuff?

"No," I said. "We cannot talk. I'm enjoying my conversation with this red Solo cup."

"No, you're not, I saw the faces you were making just now. Are you drunk?"

"Are *you?*" I said. He obviously wasn't. I don't know why I said that.

"Are you mad at me?"

"Do I look mad?" I hoped I did. Mad was better than nervous.

"Oh jeez, Elijah. I'm sorry I didn't answer your texts! I just thought maybe it would be better if we talked in person. Come on, please? It's really loud in here."

"Oh, fine," I grumbled. I put my disgusting drink down in a plant pot, and Nick wrapped his hand around my bicep to guide me to the back porch. Big hands, or else I really needed to do some push-ups. I wished I had drunk enough to make punching him seem like a reasonable decision.

"Listen," he said when we were outside, and he didn't have to yell to make himself heard. "I'm sorry about what I said, I wasn't thinking. I was trying to be funny, I guess. It came out wrong, right?"

I'd gotten so worked up over him not being there and then being there and looking like he was ready to let me down gently, I'd forgotten what I'd wanted to yell at him for. "What?"

"I didn't mean to make fun of you or anything. I mean, you were being weird and—"

"I was being weird?"

"Yeah!" He threw up his hands. "You know, you're always so deadpan about stuff, and I can never tell when you're serious! I was trying to play along!"

"Wait," I said. Wait. I was being weird. That's what I thought he'd say. The other part, not so much. "Wait, slow down. You don't know when *I'm* being serious? What about you?"

"What about me?"

"You're never serious either, you're always, like, fake-flirting with me, and it's a pain in the ass."

"Dude. I'm sorry if I insulted you, I know maybe it's a sensitive topic, but like, for what it's worth, I honestly would rather see your pecs than Aviva's breasts. Like, for real. Not that I have to see your pecs or anything if you don't want me to. Like, your face is what's important, really. Even just as friends! That's okay, too."

Maybe I was a little bit drunk after all. This conversation did not seem to be going in the direction I'd expected. "You're not making any sense, Nicholas."

"God, Eli, you're such an idiot. I'm saying, like, since we're at a party and everything, I would really like to make out with you, but if you're still mad, then I totally understand and I'm supposed to be

15

home, like, ten minutes ago anyway. And if you're straight, then, uhh, I'll just go drown myself in Steve's pool for being a doofus."

"I'm not straight," I said. "I'm so angry. I've been trying to figure out if you were gay ever since you came back from Israel. You got hot and I've been so enraged ever since. Oh my God, I thought you came out here to tell me to stop hitting on you. I'm the least straight person I know."

"Yeah? You sure about that?" He had that golden-retriever grin on his face again, like the entire universe was a gift to him personally. "Because I'm willing to fight for the title."

"So fight me."

"Is that a yes? To kissing?"

"I mean, if you're really interested in kissing a wide-hipped, nebbishy weirdo, then, like—"

"I'm very interested," he said. "But you're more Jack Kirby than nebbishy, glasses aside. J-S-Y-K."

It took all my willpower not to hide my face in my hands. How could a boy be so attractive even when speaking out loud in text abbreviations? "You want to make out with Jack Kirby? Nasty."

"Dude, it has been my life's dream. Have you seen photos of him when he was our age? Hot."

"Fine," I said, quickly. I really needed him to shut up, for the sake of preserving my dignity. "Fine. Just don't touch my pecs, please, no matter how much you were looking forward to seeing them."

He held up his hands as if to say *I'm unarmed.* "I won't, I promise! I will pretend they are vicious rodents and keep my hands at arm's length."

"Jesus Christ, Nick." I was afraid we were going to be stuck in this embarrassing conversation forever, and we'd never get to the part where we actually touched each other. "Nick. Nicholas. I really need you to make your move here. Please. I am dying."

For a second, it looked like he was going to ask a question, and I was prepared to lie down and die of gay starvation right there on Steve Anderson's back porch. I opened my mouth to tell him to please stop talking, or else stop *me* from talking, since clearly I was my own worst enemy, and that's when he finally kissed me.

And it was the best thing that had ever happened to me in my life.

Nick Cheesy Grin: *dude what were u drinking tho that shit was nasty*

Nick Cheesy Grin: *I've got like ur secondhand hangover*

Elijah Star Emoji: *omg fuck offfffff*

Nick Cheesy Grin: *lol i will 4give u in exchange for one (1) alcohol free kiss*

Elijah Star Emoji: *dang forgiveness comes cheap huh*

Nick Cheesy Grin: *only 4 u bro ;) only 4 uuuu*

Nick Cheesy Grin: <3

Gifts of Spring

Shira Glassman

*With appreciation to KD Lubeck, Brooke, and Kitty Campanile
for their assistance*

The clock in the square struck four. Beneath its face, wooden doors opened to reveal intricately-painted mechanical dancers.

Rosamund watched them from her place of safety in a forgotten, shadowed part of the café's courtyard. Enough sweet, dark beer remained in her mug to wet her lips, but she'd exhausted her potatoes and in her remote corner, the barmaids were unlikely to notice and offer more.

The meal and tower failed to provide the distraction she craved, however. The toy figures were dressed as a king and queen, and she struggled to rein her mind from going over the cliff of brooding again. Rosamund was tired: tired of royal politics, tired of running away from betrayal, and tired of running for her life. She hadn't grown up around such things, and if she'd known that her first job as a mage fresh out of magic academy would involve scheming at the highest levels of government, she might have just stayed in her village and brewed beer.

She centered herself by holding a mouthful of bittersweet doppelbock beer, tickling on her tongue, and simply experiencing her immediate environment. The Castaneanplatz was the biggest courtyard in Lilaburg, and it sprawled past government buildings, museums, and shops before culminating in a great cathedral flanked by chestnuts in full bloom. People scurried everywhere, stopping to chat or watch street performers.

The one with the biggest crowd was a sturdy yet limber man in his forties, with hair the same medium dark brown as the doppelbock in her mug. His audience left him a respectful distance, and as Rosamund looked closer she realized why—the slim objects he juggled were knives!

Gasps and applause rose from the crowd as he added two more knives to his handful and then lifted one foot off the ground. He was at least six feet tall, but he piloted his body as effortlessly as an expert rider controls a horse.

With a sweep of his arm, he scooped the flying knives from the air and placed them on the ground at his feet, on top of a rug. Next, he lay down beside them. Rosamund craned to retain her view. It was obstructed slightly by the rest of the crowd: dazzled women more forward than she and the kind of men who were always comfortable pushing their way to the best view.

His back flat against the ground, he juggled the knives again, this time directly over his face. The crowd yelped with delight. They clapped even louder when he added his feet to the trick.

The juggler leapt to stand and bowed manfully, and each knife fell to the ground with its point pinned in his rug, missing him narrowly.

"He's too good!" shouted a man in the crowd. "That's no skill, it's a wizard's trick!"

"I assure you, sir, I have no magic." The juggler spoke with the voice of a seasoned performer, confidently loud with a slight foreign lilt. "This is only the result of hard work and honest practice."

"Practice won't do what you did!" the man persisted.

"He's a cheat!" a woman agreed.

"No, madam—"

"Go on, then, prove it!" called the first man, stepping into view. He was tall, extremely thin, and wore a printer's apron.

The juggler held up his hands. "How could I prove it? I give you my word."

Another man picked up the tricornered hat in which the juggler had been collecting coins. "Easy for them that knows magic to play the working man. Ooh, we're so impressed." With this sarcastic flourish, he emptied the hat into the crowd. People scrambled for the flying money, and the man shoved the hat onto the juggler's dismayed head.

Rosamund, who had paid for her beer eons ago, crept to the periphery of the crowd, her eyes wide.

"Throw him out of the city!"

"No, in the river!"

"We don't like liars."

"I swear by Almighty God I don't know magic!" the hapless man protested. "I've been doing this all my life—"

Two men rose out of the crowd and seized him by the shoulders, and Rosamund could take no more. Swallowing her pain and fear and every impulse to hide away forever after the disaster in Schloss Gewitter, she charged up her powers and shoved herself to the front of the crowd.

"People of Lilaburg!"

The crowd fell silent with shock, dumbstruck no doubt by the unearthly glow of her eyes and mouth.

"I'm a real mage. You know we all get these at school—look." She rolled back her right sleeve to reveal a small but obvious tattoo of a shining sun. "He's not one of us." She seized the man's arm and yanked his sleeve back.

The crowd shifted uneasily as they absorbed the truth of her words.

Okay. Now she'd run out of plan. So many eyes on her, so many strangers full of anger.

She realized she still clutched the juggler's wrist, muscled and warm and full of vitality. His touch brought her to her next thought.

"There are plenty of other performers to watch," she reminded them. "I don't think any of them are mages, either."

The crowd, suspicious and confused but most likely feeling guilty because deep down they could tell she was right, fell away grumbling.

"Thank you," said the knife juggler.

"W-we should go," Rosamund stammered.

"I'm Elias, by the way."

"Rosamund." She curtseyed, her golden curls falling over her face.

He took off his hat and inspected the inside. "I'd like to buy your dinner, to thank you, but we'd have to stop at my inn first. Today's earnings seem to have been a casualty of my hecklers."

"That would be lovely. Is it far? Not that I mind a short walk. I've spent most of the day fretting in a chair."

"It may take us an hour," he admitted as he collected his knives, securing them in unobtrusive sheaths he wore at his belt. "The rooms were far cheaper beyond the city gates."

Rosamund already knew that, and her purse felt it dearly, but she had some nebulous idea that the anonymity of a populated city might protect her more should the king's forces seek her. And though her heart glowed as she observed Elias's handsome face up close, moths of fear flitted around that light. Letting the crowd tear him apart was never an option, but she'd exposed her presence to strangers and *if* the king was still looking—

On the other hand, she'd much rather have the juggler for company than her own tortured memories. "I'd enjoy the walk."

He rolled up his rug and rescued a plum-colored frock coat from within its layers. It required some dusting off before he donned it. "There. Now I'm more presentable. Pleased to make your acquaintance, Mage Rosamund."

They strolled along the cobbled streets. "How did you come to your knives?" Rosamund asked.

"Oh, I've been at this several years," said Elias. "Most cities aren't as unfriendly as this one. But I can't call it bad luck, since I've met you!"

Rosamund noticed that it wasn't an answer, but as she had stories she couldn't share without risking her life, his easy evasion was almost comfortingly familiar. "Thank you." She inclined her head slightly.

"And of yourself?" he asked. "Am I right in remembering that mages are born, not made?"

"Yes, that's right. I didn't realize what I had were magic powers at first, but when I reached thirteen, my family knew I was destined for more than Papa's brewery." Rosamund's memories were a haze before those wondrous moments when her natural abilities had revealed the young woman she'd always known she was. After that relief, she would have happily stayed in the village as a brewster, but the excitement of mage training had proved too great a temptation.

"Ah, from a brewing family!" Elias raised an eyebrow. "You must have all kinds of opinions about the beer here, then."

"Oh, I've enjoyed it," Rosamund replied. "Not like—" Never mind. *Not like the weak, watery stuff from the brewers at Schloss Gewitter.* "Not like some places. It's rich and full-flavored."

"I'll make sure to buy you a glass, then." He gestured before him. "Shall we cut through the park?"

Avenues of blooming wisteria marked the entrance, and she marveled at their beauty. "Here, let me take one for both of us." She placed a sprig in his buttonhole, and one behind her ear.

"A favorite blossom?"

"For protection."

"Ah! I see. All wisteria, or is this plant special?"

"Wisteria in general," she explained. "That rosemary plant there is for power. And—is that an apple tree beyond the footbridge? Apple blossoms bring happiness."

"They must quarrel in plant-speak after we've all gone to bed and can't hear," Elias quipped. "Power and happiness can be great enemies."

"I've learned that, too."

They stepped closer to the footbridge and Rosamund noticed two young girls, their hair in braids, peering over the railings while speaking in animated, unhappy tones. One of them tried to climb over, but the other held her back. "It's too dangerous!"

"But we'll get thrashed for sure!"

"What's the matter, little ones?" Rosamund asked.

"We've lost it in the river," blurted out the smaller girl.

"We didn't mean to!" said the other at the same time.

"Our aunt—"

"She's really Papa's aunt—"

"She'll be so angry!"

"She's always angry."

"One at a time, please," Elias requested in a calm, measured tone.

His commanding presence—or maybe his plum coat and tricornered hat—seemed to do the trick. "It was my fault," said the bigger girl. "We shouldn't have taken it out of the house."

"I'm the one who dropped it in the river," said the smaller girl.

"What have you lost, dear hearts?" asked Rosamund.

"Aunt Elsa's gold necklace," said the bigger girl.

"We were using it to play queens," the tiny one explained.

"I can swim," said Elias, "but I'd rather not spend more than a moment in; it's chilly even in springtime. Do you know where it is—can you see it?"

The girls shook their heads.

"Wait, I can help," said Rosamund. She realized she'd put a hand to his with her impulsive words, and grinned slightly as she withdrew it. "Let me listen to the water." She held out her hands over the railing. "Yes, it's here. It's nearby."

Elias had already draped his coat over the railing and was working on his shirt. As it joined its fellow, Rosamund tried not to stare at the toned muscle of his torso, shaped by years of training. She wished desperately she had a fan to hide coyly behind so that she could observe him more politely.

Rosamund forced herself to close her eyes and concentrate on the gold necklace instead of what delights she could dream up. "There. It's actually caught on the underside of the bridge."

"Good thing you picked a performer to rescue today," said Elias. He crouched beneath the railing of the bridge and tested the posts.

"What's he doing?" the bigger girl asked Rosamund.

"I'm not sure," Rosamund admitted. She stared, fascinated by more than just his physique.

All three of them gasped as he lowered himself upside down with his legs wrapped around the railings. They rushed to the side of the bridge and peered over, to see him red-faced with a glitter of gold in his triumphant grasp. "Is this your aunt's?"

The girls jumped up and down clapping. "That was wonderful!"

"Thank you so much!" The smaller girl surprised Rosamund by hugging her around the waist.

"You shouldn't take your aunt's things out of her house without asking," Elias admonished them as he placed the treasure safely within the bigger girl's cupped palm. "But you're wonderful creatures for being so willing to each take the blame instead of putting it on your sister."

The girls curtseyed and scampered off.

"N-neat trick," Rosamund stuttered, watching him put his shirt back on until her eyelashes nearly broke off in embarrassed flutters.

"Yours, too!" He shrugged himself back into the fabric. "Guess I didn't need to take this off after all."

"It was fun anyway." Rosamund gave him the tiniest rosebud of a smile before looking away again. She pawed at her gown's pink fabric, suddenly unsure what to do with her hands.

They continued past the lake that marked the park's center. Elias noted each new plant species with a gesture, his pointed eyebrows lifting in question. "The bay, then?"

Rosamund wished again for that fan. She imagined it decorated with the swans that floated like lilies on the lake. "You'll laugh at me, but it's useful for attracting women."

"I'll commit that to memory," Elias teased, "and use it to help my fellow men when they are less fortunate than I am today." Dark eyes sparkled at her, and Rosamund felt perfume in her soul. "Are there plants that attract men, too? What was in your tea this morning, lovely one?"

Rosamund pointed to an orderly garden beyond the lake. "I'm pleased if you like me, but that lavender there had nothing to do with it."

"You know *all* the plants, don't you?" Elias's eyebrows rose, and he smiled in admiration.

"The stones, too," she added promptly. "I was nearly at the head of my class."

"*Nearly?*" he asked. "Sounds like there's a story there."

Rosamund giggled. "I stayed up so late studying that I overslept and missed the first twenty minutes of the exam!"

"And today I was nearly thrown out of town for practicing *my* craft too hard." Elias shook his head, then smiled. "Well, you know your magic arts, and that's the important part, exams or no exams."

25

From the far side of the park, they emerged into a neighborhood with narrower and steeper streets than the city center from which they'd come. This was where the hill on which Lilaburg sat began to give way to the slopes that led to the city walls and lowlands beyond, and Rosamund watched her step to avoid slipping on any particularly smooth cobblestones.

Curious, narrow houses perched on these slopes, with a single storey on one side but two on another. They also often came with peculiar art to match and accent their oddities.

"The children here must have fun making up stories about the faces." Rosamund pointed to a "sun" with a bulbous nose on one house, then a gargoyle on another.

"Let's hope," said Elias. "I might have found some of them terrifying at their age."

"If I should choose one…" She considered as she walked, treating the neighborhood as her own personal gallery. "That nixie."

"That's the fairest we've seen," Elias agreed. The water nymph, or nixie, was attached to the drain spout whose water poured from a jug in her arms.

"If it rains while I'm still in Lilaburg, I would sneak back here just to see her in her full glory," said Rosamund, a little shy about revealing something so eccentric. But her heart reassured her that he would understand. "She's almost incomplete without it, and I want to see the whole artwork!"

"Ah, it's a joint effort," said Elias. "The stonemason—and God."

Rosamund's heart felt pleasantly warm at the sentiment.

The pair turned another corner, and Rosamund started slightly at the unexpected presence of two blond-haired, ponytailed young men. One had wavy locks; the other had straight and fine hair that was accompanied by a thin mustache and goatee. They were thick in conference with deeply furrowed brows, trying to move a long, thin plank of wood. Then she realized it was actually a cross.

The man with wavy hair looked up at the roof, and when she followed his gaze she saw the other half of the riddle—a religious statue.

"Did it fall out?" she asked.

The youths turned to look at her. "Yes," said the one with the mustache. They both looked incredibly embarrassed.

"It was in the crook of his arm, like this." The other one demonstrated, using his other hand to indicate its position.

"We didn't realize it wasn't fastened," the first one explained.

"Didn't realize?" Elias inquired, eyebrows raised.

The youths looked at each other. "Um."

"There may have been—"

"—arrows involved—"

"—thought it was harmless!"

The story came out piece by piece. Apparently, the two men, Maximillian and Ernst, had been trying to aim arrows through the gaps between the saint's arm and the cross. One of them, and like the little girls on the bridge they each refused to blame the other, had accidentally knocked the cross free.

"We could have been killed!" gasped Ernst, who was the one with facial hair.

"But we weren't, and that's got to count for something, right, Ernst?" said Maximillian cheerfully, though his face was blanched white in the waning sunlight.

Elias stepped back and studied the roof. "It's a shame it's not a flatter roof," he commented, "or there'd probably be an entrance on the inside that leads up, with a staircase." This roof was entirely pointy. "But I'm different, and I don't need a staircase."

"What's he talking about?" Ernst asked Rosamund.

"He's a professional acrobat," she explained. "Look!"

Elias tested his grip on the building and scrambled like a squirrel up its side. On the ground, the two youths marveled. "I can get up," he called back to them, "but not with the cross. Can you help me, Mage Rosamund?"

"Oh, absolutely!" She rushed to the task, skirts bustling about as she approached the cross and pointed her hands at it. "I'm glad you're doing that part, since I'm scared I'd bash in the poor saint's face instead of aiming it properly into the crook of his arm!"

Once under her control, the cross lifted into the air. At this sight, the men crossed themselves and stared, open-mouthed, as it slowly rose toward its former position.

She could feel its weight tugging at her being and concentrated harder. Magic could be tiring, and they'd been walking a while. It would feel good to sit down somewhere.

Rosamund's arms trembled as the blood rushed down them to her shoulders, limbs aching as she were physically carrying the heavy wood. As the cross reached the roof, she willed herself to carry it with her magic *just* a moment longer. To steel herself, she watched Elias continue his acrobatic ascent, and the distraction only sweetened her growing hunger for his touch. How skillfully he seemed to know exactly where to put his feet, and also his hands!

She wondered if he knew exactly where to put his hands in other ways.

He clambered up to the roof and swung his leg around so that he sat astride the statue like it was a horse. All he had to do was reach out into the air before him and take the cross firmly in his grasp.

"Do you have it?" Rosamund called to him.

"Yes."

Only then did she finally release it and let him place it carefully back in the crook of the saint's arm. The young men rushed to her side, and she realized she was gasping for air.

It took a few seconds for Rosamund to catch her breath. "I'm all right, but thank you." She smiled at them both.

Eventually, Elias joined them on the ground again. He wore a strange expression Rosamund could not read. "I hope we have restored your statue to its former perfection!"

"Thank you both so much." The young men bowed at them.

"I don't have to advise you to choose other targets, do I?" Elias now wore a gentle, fatherly smirk.

"We've had our shock," said Maximillian with a laugh. "At least the falling cross let us live!"

"Are you brothers?" asked Rosamund.

The men exchanged a heavy glance and gave no answer.

When Rosamund realized what that meant, her eyes immediately flew to Elias. He passed her heart's unspoken test when he jovially replied with, "Perhaps that's enough arrows for one evening. The park is lovely right now—we've just come from there. I especially recommend the lake."

"Thank you again—both of you," said Ernst.

Rosamund noted Elias fussing with his hands as they continued their descent to the city gates. "Do your hands hurt from gripping the house? I can find a plant with a balm."

"What?" He looked at his hands. "No… No, it's not that." Then he changed the subject, and Rosamund did not ask further.

Rosamund was grateful to see the city walls finally looming before them. She'd very much enjoyed walking with Elias, both in conversing and using their shared talents to help the city dwellers.

But raising the cross had brought her much pain, and her daily charms upon herself were prematurely exhausted. Already she felt the annoying itch of a beard that shouldn't be, threatening its whisper across her face. She had time yet; she'd learned to read her body well enough to pay quick attention to the warning signs.

"There, beyond the gate," Elias pointed.

Rosamund hovered, afraid to pass beyond the walls that, perhaps only superstitiously, she felt protected her from foreign kings and their mercenaries. Then she exhaled, and resolutely offered her arm to Elias. "Those I avoid expect me alone." Maybe his presence could be her disguise.

"I hope you enjoy my company for more than that." He led her through the gate.

She turned toward him, ashamed. "Do you really doubt it or are you just fishing?"

"I confess to having cast my line." Elias grinned. "You have your secrets as I have mine, but your attentions aren't one of them."

"Have I been too bold, then?" she inquired.

"Exactly bold enough," he corrected. "It is only appropriate for me to wait upon your initiative. As a mage, you outrank me in class— and also in youth."

"But you are *my* better," she countered, "in…in elegance. In dexterity. In experience."

"May I live up to all that." Elias's twinkling eyes reflected the lights of the torches that lit the entrance of his inn. "Here's where I've rented. My money is in my room."

"May I wait for you by the fireside and rest my feet?"

"Of course." He bowed to her before disappearing up the stairs.

Rosamund curled up in a chair by the hearth and unclasped her beads from her wrist. Drowning out the ordinary sounds of the innkeeper's other guests drinking, she closed her eyes and began to renew herself.

These daily rituals helped recharge her magic and reveal her to the world. The rock at the center of the bracelet wasn't magical, but a focusing stone that cleared her mind and allowed for a more profound connection with herself. A woman who wasn't magical could have worn it as nothing more than a bauble. Rosamund, on the other hand, could still perform this charm without it, just more slowly and with less grace.

She usually renewed before bedtime, but the weight of the broken statue necessitated an earlier spell. This was a lucky rest, and within the circle of motherly firelight, she breathed deeply and bathed in magic.

When Elias found her, she was refreshed and felt beautiful. "Plenty for food and drink for my charming rescuer, although we'll have to go somewhere else with an open kitchen," he said, holding up a purse proudly. Then, with dark eyes peering into hers, he added, "May we rent a carriage back to your inn for the meal?"

She knew what he was really asking. Carriages were little worlds unto themselves, completely private from the crowds in the open streets. Would she step into that little world with him, with his lips, with his hands, with all that he was?

… Oh, yes.

They walked back to the city gates and flagged down a passing coach. The coachman gallantly helped Rosamund into the back while Elias paid him.

"The inn by St. Hildegard's," Rosamund told him, when Elias realized he didn't know what to tell the driver.

The curtains closed, and as the carriage jolted to a start, she was jostled against Elias in a rustle of fabrics. His arm caught her 'round the waist, and he was close enough now that she smelled fresh soap. He must have washed up in his room.

The close contact was slowly but surely liquefying Rosamund's body. She pictured icicles in the early spring, melting into the heat they knew would only increase.

"How do you like to be kissed?"

Rosamund blinked rapidly. She'd never been asked before, so she'd never thought about it. "What are my choices?"

"Well," Eli began, "there are hungry kisses, like a beast."

"That has its appeal," Rosamund replied, "but I am not food."

"Or quick kisses, as a bird stealing a ribbon." He traced the path of a stray golden curl over her shoulder and collarbone, and she shivered and moaned softly.

"You aren't stealing," she pointed out.

"Shy kisses." He swept his fingertips, unbearably light as if he were a ghost, up the side of her face to cup her cheek with tenderness.

"You aren't afraid." She leaned forward, eager and waiting.

"Which kisses do you want, my magical beauty?"

"I wish for pleasure," breathed Rosamund into the heel of the hand that now massaged her cheek and jaw.

"I understand," said Elias. "In that case, I will draw out your pleasure." He tilted her face sideways to complement his and landed his mouth on hers in a motion calculatingly sensual.

Rosamund trembled in his arms and leaned into him. It was like jumping into a lake: to kiss him was to be surrounded on all sides. She imagined what his body would feel like against her thighs, and nearly tore apart with longing.

His lips traveled down her jaw to worship at her neck, and she let out such a startled gasp of delight that she immediately worried of the driver's sensibilities. "I will have you in my room," she decided. "But we can't go farther in this carriage."

"I understand. I hope we can dine first," Elias said. "I've had a long day and a long walk."

Rosamund nodded. "The chicken stew is very good." So were the sausages, but she was starting to suspect they contained ingredients he might not be allowed to eat. Well, she supposed she'd know in an hour or so, depending on how long they were at dinner—if what people said was true.

"If you like," Elias added, leaning close, "when we're alone, I can show you a special trick that probably only acrobats can do."

Rosamund's eyes widened as her imagination raced to figure out *that* riddle, and then fluttered shut when his tongue, already close from speaking about such intimate topics, flickered against her ear.

★ ★ ★

Rosamund's inn was much more crowded and full of noise than Elias's had been. It took both of them shouting to get their food and ale, and when it arrived, they found it easier to eat quickly without talking rather than try to converse above the din. She noticed that he asked for water as well as ale, but instead of drinking it, he used it to wash his hands.

Rosamund realized that Elias was right to insist upon food before lovemaking; she ate her chicken and barley stew with much more gusto than she'd expected to. They had, after all, walked for an hour and engaged in their little adventures with passers-by...

Each time she caught the glint of his eye above the table, it was like reliving his touch.

They finished their stew at about the same time. With a final draught of her mug, she stood. Together, they pushed through the crowd and climbed the stairs to the second floor where she'd rented her room.

Elias sat on the bed and shucked off his shoes while she found a candle and lit it from a hallway lamp. She set it on the room's simple writing desk and then closed and barred the door.

He held out his hand to her, and when she took it, he guided her onto his lap. This time as he kissed her, he draped his fingers across the modest swell of her breasts. The part that was clothed yearned to feel him without barrier; that which was skin burned and loved the attention.

As she moaned into his mouth, his fingers gracefully undid this and that until more of her breasts emerged into the candlelight. "Rarely have I seen such perfect apricots," said Elias.

"That's very pretty nonsense," she said, the words coming out in gasps.

Holding her fully supported in his improbably strong tumbler's arms, he bent his head downward to taste her. Rosamund whimpered and melted. "Is it possible to die of pleasure?"

He turned his face away from her nipple to speak. "I think coming back to life from pleasure is more likely."

She would have to consider this later when he wasn't making her body sing with a chorus of goosebumps.

Now his hands ran up and down her legs, under her skirt. She wasn't sure. She *was* sure. She decided she felt free. She wanted him so much she was scared of setting off magical sparks.

He moved her carefully off his lap and onto the bed, then took off his dress coat. Once it was laid over the bare-bones wooden headboard, he untucked his shirt. She couldn't help it—she raised one languid hand towards the stiff ridge in his breeches. She didn't touch him, but instead met his eyes with her own questioning gaze.

"Yes, magical beauty." He took her hand in his and guided it to his erection.

She massaged it for a moment of exploration, enjoying the feeling of it like new riches, before fumbling it out of the cloth.

What he had was unexpectedly sculpted and different, and he noticed her curiously blinking eyelashes as she studied him. "Well, I wasn't always as good with knives as I am now." He flashed a wicked grin beneath his raised eyebrows.

"I know what it means. I'm not as innocent as I could be!" Rosamund recalled his discomfort when carrying the giant cross.

Elias looked grave for a moment. "The crowd this afternoon—if they'd known, it could have meant trouble for other Jewish people in Lilaburg, not just me."

"I won't say anything. I promise."

He took her hands and kissed her. "And now, the trick of the acrobat. Or at least, this acrobat." He sat down on the bed, and she watched him with wide eyes as he curled himself over his own lap. She clasped her hands to her chest in shock as he bent down far enough to nudge at the tip of his own phallus with his mouth, and eventually even engulf the head completely with his lips.

"Is there no limit to your body's tricks?" she cried in wonder.

"I'd be a richer man if I could show *that* off in the Castaneanplatz."

She took him back into her hand and squeezed, and he returned his attentions to her exposed bosom. "Elias?"

"Yes?"

"Your trick—what does that feel like?" she asked.

"Would you let me show you?"

"Yes. Please."

He pushed her down gently across the bed and continued to nuzzle her breasts. Her hand was still full of him when a sudden scrape at the window drove a spike of fear through her body.

Elias reacted instantly; Rosamund seized up and tried to hide beneath him as nausea robbed her of her wits. A cloaked man had sneaked in silently through the window—the *second-story window.* But before she came to harm, Elias had leapt up and hurled two knives from his belt. "I don't want to hurt you," he growled, "but I can't let you hurt her. I don't know what you want with her, but you'll have to get through me first. And I wasn't always just an acrobat."

The intruder struggled against the knives that now pinned him to the wall. "She's a runaway from the court of King Bertram at Schloss Gewitter in the north," sneered a voice Rosamund recognized in a blood-chilling moment—the man from the angry mob in the Castaneanplatz, the one who'd dressed as a printer. "There's a purse of gold on her head. Everyone else thought she went to France, but I followed her here and finally tracked her down."

Elias shot Rosamund a glance. "Is this true?"

She nodded, shivering violently. "Help. Me." With shaking hands, she wrapped his jacket around her naked chest.

The mercenary wrenched his shoulders forward until Elias charged back to his side and aimed a third knife at his throat.

Rosamund unfolded her legs and found the floor. Unsteady on her feet, she stood anyway. "No, wait. I can...his memory." She took a deep breath.

Elias shot her half a glance. "Are you sure?"

She nodded spasmodically. "Our souls don't need this violence." *And I will never be the same woman if someone kills in my name*, she realized.

"Do it quickly," he muttered. "My knives are only so far into the wall."

Rosamund held out both her hands and breathed in and out in a deep, even rhythm. "You can take a different path. Return to the village of your childhood. The woman with the...goat farm?... sheep?... goat farm is still there, and she'd love to see you again."

The bounty hunter's eyes grew black as his pupils expanded to cover the entire surface. When the whites returned, he blinked at her in bafflement. "Where am I?"

Rosamund looked at Elias. "You can take your knives back now."

"Are you sure?"

"Yes, quickly!"

As Elias bustled the confused man out of the room, a creeping thought descended on Rosamund like a blanket. She could erase herself from *his* mind too—he already knew she was a fugitive now, and that there was money on her head. His arms were the first place she'd felt truly happy since she'd been betrayed by her employers and fled from the home she'd trusted. But he was also the one weak spot in her remaining hidden. Without him, she could go to another city and be anonymous again.

She looked at her fingers, feeling her seconds of choice tick away to zero.

Elias barred the door and turned to face her where she stood clutching the edges of his purple dress-coat around herself like a child in the rain. Almost unconsciously, her hands drifted up into the same position again, the spell welling within her, trying to protect her and erase her indiscretions.

But like a cold wind, she remembered the misery of her loneliness until that afternoon. What was safety if she was miserable—if she did not *live*?

"Oh." The sound fell as a gasped choke from her lips as her outstretched hands clasped his.

"Roseleh," he cooed into her ear as he held her close to him, his strong hands massaging her back. "You don't have to tell me what that was about, but—"

"No, I want to."

"If it's not too upsetting."

They sat down on the bed together, and he kneaded her palm and fingers as she talked. She told him how excited she'd been, fresh out of magic academy, to be honored with a post in a royal court. Of how the king had been pleased with her obedience and the queen with her companionship and conversation. And then, of how both had tried to trick her into becoming a pawn in their deadly, scheming games against each other.

"They both tricked me," she sobbed. "I was their friend. I looked up to the king. I was the queen's confidant."

"You were too sweet and too good to go along with their real plans," said Elias.

Rosamund nodded, wiping away her tears. "I had no idea. And when I found out, I handled it all badly, and now they both want me dead."

"That man said everyone else was looking for you in France, right?"

Rosamund nodded again.

"So you should be safe here. Or if we go farther east."

"We?"

Elias looked into her eyes. "If you're enjoying my company enough."

"Can you question it?" she cried, her voice breaking. "This is the first time since I fled that I've been happy."

"And we make such a good team. Three times in one day, your magic and my skills have paired to excellent ends."

She smiled broadly and then cast her eyes down. "When we lay down together, it will be four."

"Are you still ready for all that?" He caressed her hair.

She squeezed his thigh. "I want to feel alive."

Gently, he lay aside the jacket from her shoulders and kissed away the hurt and pain from her heart.

Wishing On The Perseid

Kay C. Sulli

Everyone always assumed it was Zach Johnson's first time in the forest. Maybe it was because of the color of his skin, the Southern accent, or the lack of regard for outdoor status symbols like two-hundred-dollar fleece jackets and five-hundred-dollar hiking boots. He didn't know, and on this trip, he was determined not to care. It was the first time he'd been able to wrangle a vacation in years, the gap between finishing his master's program and starting a PhD the perfect opportunity. Considering that he was headed for Colorado State University in a month's time, the refuge of the Colorado mountains called to him. It was the middle of August and the flocks of families had flown back towards the cities they came from, leaving Rocky Mountain National Park feeling nearly empty. It left space for the ranging twenty-somethings and the retired seeking an adventure before the snow flew.

It was on Zach's second evening in the Moraine Park campground when he first saw Ranger Ryan Jenkins. Zach had stumbled upon the amphitheater on accident, wandering the footpaths of the campground through the sweet-smelling red trunks of Ponderosa Pines and nearly tripping over a sturdy sagebrush that was hiding in a patch of tall grass. The audience was spread out among the wooden benches, only a few sitting close to the man. A dim PowerPoint displaying a picture of a tree glowed on a screen behind him. Ryan had looked up at him, smiled, and continued on with his talk. For a brief moment, Zach had considered racing right back into the woods, but that smile caused him to sink onto one of the benches in the very back. The smile had been intriguing, friendly, and absolutely charming.

By the end of the presentation, Zach could only remember a few facts about the various trees that Ryan had spoken of, but he could remember the way the gray uniform shirt had pulled across the ranger's chest and how the forest-green trousers rose and shifted as he gestured to one thing or another. He had watched a brown curl escape from beneath his flat hat brim and brush the bridge of a sunburned nose. Zach had been mesmerized by the exposed throat and just the hint of his undershirt peeking through the V at his neck. After watching him for the duration of the talk, he concluded that they were also around the same age.

People filtered out of the amphitheater at the end, leaving only Zach and a pair of young women, probably a few years younger than Zach's twenty-eight. The women hurried up to Ranger Ryan, giggling. Zach had been drawn down the steps himself, although he told himself that it was only because he wanted to take another route back to his campsite.

Ryan was working on something inside a wooden box, turning off the projector and packing up a computer, when the young women got to him.

"Hey, Ranger," the girl began. "We were wondering if you would want to come out for a drink."

Ryan seemed stunned for a moment, as though he'd had an answer about trees or where to go hiking ready, but no response for an invitation out. He stood up and cleared his throat, "I'm sorry, but I have plans tonight."

A brush off, Zach thought. "Tomorrow?" the second woman asked, a hopeful tone in her voice.

An awkward smile and a shrug. "Gotta work." The two seemed to take the hint and walked out of the amphitheater, disappointment in their gaits. Ryan watched them for a moment and turned around to get back to work. He saw Zach and smiled. "Can I help you?"

"Yeah, uh, I just wanted to say your presentation was really good." Or rather watching you was very good, Zach added in his head. Zach offered him a hand. "Zachary Johnson from Alabama."

"Thanks." Ryan seemed genuinely pleased. His hand was warm in Zach's, and he made no move to squeeze and then pull back quickly. "I'm Ryan Jenkins from Colorado, but you would know that if you hadn't been late to my talk." The grin widened, and the joke lit up Ryan's light-brown eyes. Zach knew immediately he was being teased. Dare he hope it was a flirtation.

"Well, if I had known you were speaking I would have sat in the front row." Up close, Ryan's smile was even more pleasing.

"How long are you in the park for?"

"Two weeks."

"I'm leading a hike tomorrow. Starts at the Fern Lake Trailhead, going up to the falls. Starts at nine."

"I'll be there," Zach replied, quick on the draw, mentally canceling any other tentative plans he'd made for the following day.

"Awesome, see you then." Ryan gave him one last smile before pulling his hand away and ducking back into the box. He gathered up the rest of his things before heading towards the parking lot. Zach watched him go.

Even if Ryan was just being friendly, Zach told himself it was worth a shot to see what that lingering handshake meant.

"Am I the only one?" Zach said, startling Ryan, who had been staring at his watch. The day had broken with clouds filling the sky, the threat of rain keeping most close to camp or headed into town where shelter was abundant. Ryan already had a clear piece of plastic stretched over his hat, but no other admission to the threat of rain was in evidence. His uniform showed a few specks of drops on the gray shoulders, but the rest seemed pristine. Zach might have taken the opportunity to observe him before speaking up.

"Seems so. My boss told me to cancel, but it was up to me and…" He looked away and blushed. Zach could feel heat of his own creeping into his body, and going decidedly the other direction.

"And?"

"And, well, I was kinda hoping you would come. I mean…" The bluster was hidden beneath the brim of his hat as he talked to Zach's old Army boots that he'd inherited from his father. Zach let the smile creep onto his face. He had not imagined the lingering handshake. "…It's just I noticed you when you came to my talk last night."

Zach felt his heart drop a little. Voice flat, he said, "Because I looked different."

Ryan looked up, panic on his face. "No! It's just you watched me so intently. Maybe I wanted to know more about that." His mouth quirked in a hopeful smile shared between the empty dirt lot and Zach. It was Zach's turn to blush.

"Well, you know, you just knew so much about trees I couldn't help but be fascinated." He inadvertently gestured to Ryan's entire body, and his mind suddenly drifted to a tree analogy he should not be thinking. Rain started to splatter his shoulders, threatening to cool him off. Ryan's cheeks were still pink as he laughed.

"If you want to hike, the offer is still open, although it's looking more and more like we're gonna get soaked."

"A little water never hurt anybody."

The rain began to fall in earnest halfway to their destination. Thunder cracked overhead, chasing away the sudden brightness that lightning had just thrown against the wet trunks of the trees and the glistening granite faces of the rocks. Ryan led them to one of the backcountry ranger cabins, ushering Zach inside first and pulling the door shut behind them. There was a little propane heater in one corner, which Ryan flicked on. The humming soon producing warmth that Zach huddled near in a decades-old wooden chair.

Zach had told himself he was going to be fine, his rain jacket adequate over his light long-sleeved shirt. It had been too long since he'd been in the Rockies, and he had somehow forgotten how low the temperature could drop even in the summer. As determined as he was to not let Ryan see him shivering, he was losing that battle.

"Here." A green sweater dangled in front of Zach's face. "Sorry if it smells, haven't washed it in a while, but it should warm you up."

Zach took it in his hands, feeling the wool. He thought of protesting that he did not need it, but the truth was, he did. He shoved off his cold, wet raincoat and draped it over the back of his chair. He shrugged into the offered garment, finding it a little too small but comfortable. A male smell clung to it—Ryan's. He took the opportunity of the other man's back being turned to press his nose into it, remembering their conversations as they'd walked up the trail. Their talk had started off with what was probably Ryan's standard ranger spiel, but had shifted into more casual talk and jokes.

A voice squawked over the radio and Ryan answered it, explaining that he had taken shelter with a visitor and would notify dispatch when he was headed back. That done, he shrugged out of his own rain shell, dropping the dark green fabric on the back of one of the other aged chairs and settling into it. He reached down to pull at the laces of his boots.

"Do you mind? My feet got wet."

Zach shook his head and kicked off his own shoes in response, soon settling his white-socked feet next to Ryan's black wool socks near the heater. Zach watched him out of the corner of his eye as Ryan seemed to thoughtfully consider the red coils of the heater. His hair had been crushed beneath the hat, leaving some of the strands straight, while those that had not been so confined curled around the tops of his ears. Some stubble clung to his cheeks beneath his tan, as though it considered becoming a beard but could not commit. A brief meeting of light and dark brown eyes sent both back to contemplation.

"When I was a little kid, I used to wish on stars a lot," Ryan said, shifting in his chair to make himself more comfortable.

"Me too. Never worked, though."

"What were you wishing for?"

"Get out of the little town I was born in. There was a lot of crap, baggage, you know. I wanted more than a factory job. I was lucky that my mom and dad wanted that for me too. What about you?"

"For a friend. You might not believe this, but I was a really shy kid, wouldn't talk to anyone." He shrugged. "I can still be that way sometimes."

"But you stand in front of people and talk all day."

"Well, sometimes we're the shyest and loneliest people in the park."

Thunder cracked, cutting off Zach's reply. The rain pounded the roof so hard, hail joining the cacophony, that all attempts at conversation were lost. It left them settled in silence, inches from each other, every fiber of Zach's being wanting to reach out and take Ryan's hand in his own.

Arriving back at his camp, Zach piled the dry firewood he'd stashed beneath the bear box. He pulled the park newspaper out of his car, pausing for a moment to look at the picture of a waterfall. Was that the one they had been hiking to see? Probably not, Zach thought. There were dozens of waterfalls, maybe even more. He crumpled up a few pages to use them for fire starter. A few of the logs on the bottom were damp, but with a few false starts he was able to get a fire going. His camp chair had been folded that morning so it was blissfully dry when he sat down, settling his boots near the fire. The fire looked like it crackled between his feet. He watched the flames dance, pulling the toes of his boots away when he was afraid the rubber would melt.

"It doesn't mean anything," he said aloud to himself. Zach wanted to believe it. Ryan was probably just being nice—that was what rangers did, right? They were in the business of talking to people all day every day. What had Ryan said? They "facilitated experiences" or something like that. That was probably what it was. It sounded really clinical though, "facilitated". Was that really what he thought he did all day?

The logs crackled, sending up a wave of sparks. The sky was darkening now, the campfires popping up in the other nearby sites. Zach considered the other people there in the campground. They were in their own little rings of campfire, the woodsmoke soaking into their clothes as they cooked dinner on a fire or a nearby gas stove. It only took a whiff of the rain crisp air to smell the propane. Ryan would probably smile at all of them as well.

But would Ryan mean it?

That look. The confession of wishing on stars. Neither seemed rehearsed. It didn't sound like something he said to everyone he took out into the woods. Ryan had been genuine. He'd really meant what he'd said. The silence he'd left dangling was filled with so much. Zach could still feel the warmth from Ryan's skin only a few inches away. What would have happened if he had just reached out and touched him?

Zach leaned back, craning his neck to look up at the sky. The rain clouds had been carried off, leaving only wisps behind that made black streaks across the glowing night sky. For a moment, Zach could do nothing but admire the Milky Way tumbling across the sky. Millions of stars in the far arm of the galaxy. In the face of all that, what was one human taking a chance? In a few days, meteors would dart across the sky, at least that's what Ryan said. What would happen if two of them collided? Would the streak be even brighter?

With the fire crackling at his feet and the stars blinking overhead, Zach decided. He needed to find out exactly what Ryan meant by wishing on stars. He wanted to know if he was asking him to help him out of his loneliness.

Every time Ryan gave a talk or a hike over the next week and a half, Zach was there, although never as blessedly alone as he had been on that first hike in the rain and the companionable silence in which it ended. They would chat before and after each one, Ryan standing close. It could be a sign, but Zach wasn't sure. Despite his indecision, his time to leave was coming soon and he knew he needed to say something. If he didn't speak up, he would explode with the not knowing what could happen between them. He sat in the back of the amphitheater considering how he would approach the subject, when a pair of green trousers ended up in his vision, covering hips that he had spent far too much time observing.

"So, I think you should come to my cabin tonight," Ryan said.

The statement was delivered so abruptly that "What?" tumbled out of his mouth before he could fully process the words.

Ryan looked suddenly embarrassed, as if he had been bold about the wrong thing. "Remember, we were talking about the Perseid meteor shower two days ago. It's supposed to peak tonight. You were saying we should have some beers and watch it. I don't get off until the visitor center closes at eight, but…" The sentence trailed off, leaving space for Zach to answer and fill the space.

Zach gave him a smile, his heart beating faster. "Yeah, I'll come by around eight thirty."

Ryan's smile brightened. "See you then." He left Zach with directions and went back to work.

★ ★ ★

Zach spent the rest of the day in agony, wondering if it was going to be beers between friends or something more. He had nearly talked himself into believing that the blushes, flirtations, and all moments of closeness had been his imagination. He got so nervous about it that he showed up on Ryan's front porch twenty minutes early. If a car had not been parked out front, Zach would have wondered if he'd beaten the ranger home. The place was small and looked like it had been built near the turn of the twentieth century. The fanciful notion of being a Buffalo Soldier in the wilderness crossed his mind, something about comrades in arms, but he brushed it away.

He stood there, his hand raised to knock, butterflies rioting in his stomach and freezing him to the spot. The door opened—Ryan must have heard him pull up—and he stood there, his hat off, curls crushed from their confinement, the first few buttons of his uniform shirt undone.

"Sorry I'm early."

"No, come in," Ryan said, smiling. He pushed open the screen door, holding it open for Zach. The way he stood in the door, and the narrowness of the historic frame, meant Zach had to turn sideways and slide through. His chest bumped against Ryan's, setting his nerves on fire. He knew then there was no way he was making it through a platonic night.

The place was sparse, the interior a studio with a kitchenette on one wall, a door leading to a narrow bathroom in another, a single full-sized bed shoved up against one of the walls. Ryan's flat hat was discarded on top of a lamp on a narrow bedside table. A small dining table was to Zach's immediate right, and he dropped off the six-pack there.

The screen door clanged shut. Zach turned to see Ryan looking at him, interest in his gaze. Zach swallowed, his eyes tracing the lines of Ryan's body where he leaned against the inner door, buttons undone on his shirt, trousers still pressed, although nothing was on his feet. Silence stretched between them.

Ryan cleared his throat and took a step closer, his body reaching past Zach's. "What did you bring?" He was close, pressing between the door frame and Zach's own body. Now. Zach leaned into him and pressed his mouth against Ryan's. The reaction was immediate, Ryan's arms coming around him pulling him close. Ryan kissed him back in force. The attraction had definitely not been in Zach's imagination.

Taking a shaky breath, Zach leaned back. "Should we shut the door?"

Ryan chuckled. "We could be out there rolling in the dirt and no one would see us."

"Well, it might be a hell of a lot more comfortable in here."

A grin. "Do you see me arguing? I've been dying for you to touch me since you first stumbled into my talk." His arms tightened around Zach's waist, pressing their hips together. Zach sunk his fingers into the gray fabric of the shirt and pulled him closer, leading him towards the bed in the corner. Ryan came willingly enough, and when Zach turned and pushed the other man down, he knew he had made the right call. The grey shirt was wrinkled, another button had slipped out from the rough treatment, and the green-clad legs invitingly spread, just waiting for Zach to come between them.

"Hell, you should have said something sooner, boy."

"I'm twenty-six."

"Younger than me, makes you a boy."

Ryan raised his arms above his head, stretching his body out along the bed where Zach still stood at the foot. "Fair enough," he said, "as long as it means you're gonna fuck me all the same."

"Well, now that I know you're old enough," he teased. At that, Ryan hooked his legs around the back of Zach's and yanked him forward. Zach caught himself on his hands and was soon pulled into another kiss by Ryan. The kiss was rough and sent his entire body burning. He enjoyed the push and pull for several minutes until he could no longer ignore the badge poking his chest. He gripped it in his fingers. "This has gotta go."

They fumbled with the buttons of Ryan's shirt for a few moments, getting in each other's way, but soon the fabric was tossed to the floor, and a moment later the white tank beneath. The eager expression on Ryan's face made Zach want to yank everything else off him as soon as possible, but he wanted to take him slow, feel every inch of him for as long as possible, his time in the mountains almost up. The flat hat on the lamp caught his eye, and he grabbed it. Ryan looked at him curiously as Zach held it in his hands. Then he dropped it onto Ryan's head, covering his eyes.

"What are you—?"

"Just go with it."

Ryan shrugged and blindly reached for him as Zach pulled off his T-shirt. He let Ryan's fingers run over his chest before abruptly scooting back out of reach. A frustrated sound came from the head of the bed. Zach chuckled as the complaints were silenced by his fingers along the hem of the perfectly ironed trousers. He loosened the belt and pulled it slowly through the loops, Ryan lifting his hips to make it an easier task. Leather tooled into the shape of pinecones joined the other clothing on the floor with a clank of metal buckle. Without words, Zach pressed his face to the front of the forest-green pants he'd been examining for the better part of the last week. He could smell Ryan through the fabric, feel the heat of him through the wool. He pressed his mouth against him, breathing out.

"Zach…"

Zach didn't say anything, keeping his face pressed against him and reaching one hand to slide slowly across Ryan's stomach. The other man twitched, his hands catching Zach's arm and pulling his fingers to his mouth. The warm, wet of a tongue on the palm of his hand released a groan from his mouth. One handed, he struggled with the hook and button at the top of the pants, soon realizing he needed his other hand. He reluctantly pulled it back from Ryan's warm mouth and made quick work of the green fabric and the checkered boxers beneath it. He took the other man in, and Ryan pushed the ranger hat over his forehead to raise an eyebrow.

"I'm never going to be able to attend one of your talks again. I'm gonna be thinking dirty thoughts any time I see you in that hat."

"You mean you weren't already?" Zach matched Ryan's grin with his own. He lowered himself and between Ryan's thighs, brushing his cheek against the other's hard sex, and he enjoyed the look of pure want that crossed Ryan's face.

"Well, now I'll have experience for the fantasy."

He barely had the patience to place the condom over Ryan's cock, he wanted him so badly. His mouth followed the rubber as soon as it could, his throat filling with heat as his ears filled with moans. The hairs on Ryan's legs scratched his shoulders. He made a study of the man he'd been thinking about who, not that dominated every thought since he first saw him. Ryan was not unlike the land he lived on, rough and rugged, holding close to its secrets, beautiful from afar. However, when he managed to get close and examine, he found so much more beauty in the details.

Ryan shook after his climax, heavy pants filling the small room. Zach could feel his own body struggling for satisfaction as he crawled up onto the bed and pulled Ryan's back to his front, holding him as he came down from the sexual high. The ranger hat was soon banished back to the nightstand as the hard brim knocked Zach in the nose, pulling a laugh from Ryan's throat. Zach buried his nose into the back of Ryan's neck and just breathed in his sent, his fingers roaming over him, Ryan's hand reaching back and lying flat against Zach's still-clothed ass. Ryan's fingers tightened.

"Why are you still wearing this?"

"Was a little busy."

"Hmmm." Soft breaths sounded for a few minutes, Ryan's seemingly boneless body fitting against Zach's chest. Ryan was slighter than Zach would have guess from beneath the uniform, but the lines of his body were hard from being outdoors most days. He amused himself tracing the tan line from the ranger shirt on Ryan's arm halfway down. Twisting, Ryan pressed his mouth to Zach's, the cleverness of his tongue making Zach ache for him even more. Their lips still close, Ryan whispered, "I want you to fuck me."

"You ready?" Ryan pulled Zach's hand to his groin, his body stirring again.

"Get those pants off you and…" he pushed his tongue into Zach's mouth in demonstration. "I'll be ready in no time."

Zach slid his remaining clothing down as fast as he could, returning to the warm body in the bed, kissing and caressing him into readiness. His fingers pressed against Ryan's ass, just waiting for the signal.

It came with a fumble for the drawer on the bedside table and the thrust of materials into Zach's hands. Ryan rolled over onto his stomach, a ready invitation. A funny story Ryan had told him about elk mating rituals jumped into his head, making him chuckle.

Ryan's voice came muffled from the blankets. "What, you don't like my ass?"

"Oh, I like your ass just fine. I was only hoping you weren't gonna run away from me like a white-assed elk."

Ryan laughed into the pillows. "And here I thought you were just imagining me naked instead of listening to me talk."

"I can multitask."

"I can't speak for the elk, but they are probably just making sure they really like what the bull has to offer." Ryan looked at him over his shoulder with a dirty smirk. He raised an eyebrow, silently asking Zach what was taking so long.

Zach finished his preparation, and Ryan breathed into the pillow as he positioned himself, pushing in slowly. They moved together, his body pressed up against Ryan's, his sweat mingling with Ryan's between his shoulder blades. He pressed his face to the ranger's back and quickened his thrusts at the sounds the man made. He held his breath, listening to Ryan's heart pound and a satisfied groan rumble through his chest as he released for a second time. A few more thrusts and Zach collapsed on top of him, warmth and the tingle of his own release coursing through his body.

He must have drifted off after, he realized, waking to find the cabin filled with darkness, dim starlight seeping through the open windows. Ryan breathed rhythmically beside him, relaxed in sleep. From what little light there was in the room, he could see they had made a mess of it, clothes strewn about and the blankets haphazardly wrapped around them in half-asleep attempts for some warmth for their cooling skin.

The room still smelled of their exertions, and the memory warmed Zach as he pressed a kiss into Ryan's bare shoulder. A sleepy noise of waking crept from the other man. "Hmmm?"

"We should probably get cleaned up. You can go first if you want."

"Or my shower could fit both of us. You are not sneaking out on me."

"Why would I do that?"

"That's what they always do."

"They?"

"Everyone I try to get close to."

Zach turned Ryan's face toward him. "I promise I will be here when the sun rises."

Ryan looked into his eyes, barely visible in the dark. "All the same, I would rather have you in the shower with me."

"Sure thing."

★ ★ ★

The shared Ryan's lone towel to dry off after the hot shower and sweet kisses they had shared. Zach felt a warmth that had nothing to do with sex or desire spreading through his chest—dressing together felt companionable. Domestic. He understood how Ryan felt, hoping that the other person would still be there once the sun rose.

He was about to say something when a flash lit up the space. "What was that?" he said, his heart pounding.

Ryan pushed out the screen door and looked up, "Looks like the show is about to start! Grab a blanket!" Zach back through the door with the comforter from the bed. Grabbing his hand, Ryan pulled him a little farther out into the meadow, taking the blanket and spreading it out on the grass. He stretched out on top of it and Zach followed suit, resting pressed to Ryan's side shoulder to hip. Another flash in the sky: a falling star, a meteor. One after another, they flashed across the sky, leaving bright tails behind them. The sky was so clear that he could see satellites tracking their way through the blackness, rushing faster than any star. Every flash brought a gasp of excitement from Ryan. Zach glanced over to see him beaming at the night sky.

He turned back to the sky, enjoying nature's spectacle and wondering if wishes made on a pieces of falling, burning space rock could come true.

"I wish I could see you again after I leave," Zach said softly, not sure if he wanted Ryan to hear. "I have to leave to head down to Colorado State to start school soon."

Silence. Maybe Ryan had not heard after all.

"You're going to CSU?" Ryan said, breaking the quiet.

"Yeah, grad program in engineering."

Ryan laughed, his voice seeming unnaturally loud in the quiet of the night. More flashes across the night sky lit up his face: he looked relieved.

"Here I was wishing the same thing. I'll be starting my second year down there in natural resources."

Zach couldn't believe his luck, and he pulled Ryan to him and kissed him beneath the summer meteor shower, so grateful that he would not have to leave his ranger behind. Wishing on stars had finally worked for them after all.

Hunt and Peck

Teresa Theophano

Mr. Fitzpatrick taught my fellow eighth graders and me how to type in a dank room full of old-fashioned typewriters. He stood before us to model the precise way in which one should hold one's hands—the fingers not too crooked, the wrists lifted properly. Then he'd prowl around the room, towering over each of us in turn, maybe to make sure we were doing our best to prevent the eventual onset of carpal tunnel syndrome.

"F-F-F space, D-D-D space, S-S-S space," he'd intone, cradling a steaming paper cup and emitting coffee breath with every word. He put the cup down only when he needed both hands to demonstrate the finer points of creating a "mailable" letter—that is, acceptable for the purposes of dropping into a mailbox. A middle schooler had to take great care indeed to avoid appalling the recipient of this hypothetical missive with glaring typos, erroneous margins, or inconsistent spacing.

Now is the time for all good men to come to the aid of the party, he had us type over and over again. I liked to rebel silently by substituting, *Now is the time for all good girls to fight for their right to party.*

The scent of old coffee hovered in a cloud long after Mr. Fitzpatrick ambled away from my desk. Still, in spite of that dull typing drill we had to keep practicing in the airless room, I found that I looked forward to class each day. I met with little success in any extracurricular activity that involved a team or a ball, but I was a natural at typing. As the end of the semester approached, I cheerfully zoomed my fingers around the typewriter keys during our timed tests. Mr. Fitzpatrick paused when he approached my desk to return my graded paper on our very last day of class.

"I've never seen scores like this, Ms. Sommerville." Despite the flatness of his voice—not an emotive guy, that one—I beamed. We weren't even having a contest, yet it seemed that for the first time in my life, I had won.

And soon I began to win *big*. It wasn't long after earning my A+ in Mr. Fitzpatrick's class and finishing out middle school that I entered my hometown's annual Summer Typing Challenge. When I was awarded my first trophy, I knew I was onto something important. Mom and Dad encouraged me, buying me a secondhand Smith Corona I was allowed to keep in my room and letting me stay up past ten p.m. each night practicing.

I began entering regional competitions and celebrating local triumphs. I took our whole county by storm with an upset to the winner of every contest in the past five years. My photo appeared in the *Turnpike Times*—my brother was so jealous! At my first South Jersey intermural, I beat out those rich kids from Blueberry Grove, and the infrequent and frowned-upon but exciting competitors from the "wrong side of the tracks" over in Bayview.

It was at my second regional contest that I found myself sneaking glances at one of those competitors. He was a Bayview kid—a rough-looking boy in need of a haircut. He smoked cigarettes! I mean, it's not that I ever saw him do it, but the tattered denim jacket he wore even in that broiling summer we had, and perhaps his skin itself, exuded a stink of stale smoke. His sharp cheekbones, almond-shaped eyes, and perpetual scowl made him stand out like a sore thumb. I didn't understand how he could be part of something as wholesome as typing, attracting as it did so many overachievers and rich kids whose parents could afford private touch-typing tutors.

I was in love.

The cute boy didn't make eye contact with anyone—not even his own team members, let alone me. My team beat Delmar; the Bayview team beat Blueberry Grove. And then we faced off against each other. I didn't get to talk to him in that round, of course—it's not a time for chit-chat—but I kept him in my peripheral vision during each timing. I couldn't help noticing that my classmate, gossipy Caroline, seemed to be eyeing him as well. The score was close, and my teammates looked as nervous as I felt. One of them stage-whispered at me, "We need to take those dirtbags down!" I didn't think that was very nice. I mean, sure, the girls from the Bayview team wore entirely too much eyeliner, and each had probably emptied an entire can of Aqua Net into her hair, but that didn't mean they were dirty or cheap.

In the end, it was close—but the ref called out, "Bayview takes first place!" and I saw Caroline's face fall. Disappointment that we hadn't beaten them at all, let alone by the landslide we'd anticipated, weighed heavily in my chest, seeming to squeeze my heart into a tiny ball. We'd come in second.

But all was not lost. I'd see that adorable, smoky-smelling boy at the third and final regional—a tiebreaker—in just two weeks.

I planned my outfit throughout those interminable fourteen days, changing my mind every few hours and finally settling on my favorite pale-pink, off-the-shoulder sweatshirt dress. I'd worried it might be too risqué for the occasion, but deep down I knew I'd be glad I'd chosen it once Bayview Boy caught a glimpse of me.

He looked every bit as dreamy and sullen as I remembered, and regarded me impassively as we faced each other before our first round, giving my hand only the briefest of squeezes during the mandatory handshake that preceded our match. But I noted the warmth of his palm and how firm his grasp was, even while his hands were on the small side. His fingers were tapered, elegant; I might have expected to see dirt under a Bayview boy's nails or bike grease staining his knuckles, but those hands were surprisingly clean and almost delicate.

It turned out that his name was Bri. Short for Brian, I guessed. At my school, there were almost as many Brians among the boys as there were Kims and Jens among the girls. Surely it was the same at his, since he lived only one town over. He probably went by Bri to set himself apart, the way I did by spelling my name Khrystyna.

I smiled encouragingly at him, even though he was technically the (hot) enemy. "Good luck," I managed to squeak out, and felt annoyed at myself when I realized a blush was spreading across my cheeks. Why was I acting so ridiculous in front of this stupid boy who wasn't even on my team? This wasn't like me at all—the crude, zitty creatures at my own middle school were of no interest to me— and I couldn't let my strange reaction to Bri detract from my focus.

He made a kind of grunting sound, his gaze directed at the floor. So rude—he couldn't even meet my eyes! I had to stop mooning over his good looks. Well, we'd see what kind of an opponent he turned out to be when the stakes were this high.

I creamed him in the first round. He beat me fair and square in the second. The third found me a bundle of nerves. I *had* to overcome him in this tie-breaker—if I didn't make it past this stage of the regionals, I'd be done for, a has-been, just another entry in the annals of that *Who's Who in Typing* yearbook of mediocrity.

I couldn't let that happen! I mustered all my focus, imagining Mr. Fitzpatrick beaming at me and saying "You can do this, Khrystyna," in something other than a monotone for the first time.

"Thanks, Mr. F.," I murmured. Bri looked at me strangely.

Okay, I hadn't meant to say that aloud. But my technique worked: I beat Bri by a solid twelve points in the final round. I breathed a sigh of relief when our timings were announced, and the auditorium erupted in applause. Bri slunk out just as I caught sight of my parents and my best friend, Katie, standing up in the bleachers, cheering wildly. I don't think I'd ever seen my dad look so proud! Mom rushed over and pressed a lush bouquet of gerbera daisies into my arms. "I know they're your favorites." She kissed my cheek.

"Thanks, Mom! Is it okay if I go out with some friends after this to celebrate? I promise I'll be home before nine thirty to practice." Mom nodded, and Dad told me they'd see me at home later.

I guessed Bri was a sore loser, and I couldn't deny feeling a little disappointed at his disappearance. Katie flanked me as I stepped outside of the auditorium—and immediately caught sight of beautiful Bri, leaning against the wall. It looked like he was waiting for me to emerge. I knew that Katie noticed, and instantly my nerves kicked into action, my breath catching in my throat. "I've got to pee," Katie suddenly announced, and catching my eye meaningfully, she took hold of my congratulatory bouquet and strode off toward the girls' room.

"Hey," Bri muttered in my direction.

"Oh, hi." I wanted so badly to sound nonchalant.

He still wasn't making eye contact with me, but his voice was gentler and more high-pitched than I expected when I finally heard him speak an entire sentence. "Um, congratulations. You were really good in there."

I felt myself starting to perspire lightly. He hadn't grunted or muttered this time—instead, he'd complimented me! I hoped the armpits of my dress weren't growing dark with my sweat and that my hair wasn't too flat by now; I'd sprayed it generously before leaving the house. I licked my dry lips and managed to say "Thanks."

He gulped visibly and, while he still looked down, a string of words came out of his mouth very quickly. I wasn't quite sure I'd understood the string correctly, it seemed so miraculous: "Do you want to catch a movie this weekend?"

"Uh. Um. I, well, I have plans Friday night," I lied, "but maybe we could meet Saturday for a matinee?"

He looked up at last, his beautiful, deep-set eyes meeting mine. His whole face broke into a grin, and—how could I not have realized this until now?!—I saw that Bri wasn't a surly guy at all. She was a shy tomboy! "Yeah, that'd be great."

What was I going to tell my friends?

I'd told Mom I was meeting up with Katie in front of the Glenwood Five Movie Theater, and she dropped me off twenty minutes before the movie was set to begin so that I could supposedly get tickets and popcorn for us. "Katie's mom will drop me off later," I assured her, and I've always been such a good girl that there was no way she would become the least bit suspicious.

I felt guilty—but only slightly—lying to her. After all, Mom wouldn't object to me seeing a movie with a new girlfriend. Just a friend, I told myself. She's a girl. It doesn't matter how excited you are to see her or how much she looks like a hot guy. She will be a new friend.

Whatever Bri was, I felt like my whole being lit up when she approached, and that had to mean this was right. Plus she was really sweet now that she'd started speaking to me in full sentences, and insisted on paying for me at the box office. "Don't worry about it," she assured me, "I have some babysitting money."

My look of surprise must have registered.

Bri chuckled. "There's a couple with a little kid on the edge of Glenwood, and they trust me. I'll tell you more about it later."

We chose seats toward the back of the theater. I was too excited by her presence to eat the popcorn she'd bought us or to pay much attention to the movie. It was called *Less Than Zero,* and I know it had something to do with drugs and the guy from *Pretty in Pink* who didn't end up getting or staying very famous, even though he had a nice smile.

At one point, I glanced at her; I'd felt her eyes on me, and when our gazes met, my cheeks heated up. She smiled slightly and then I looked away. Now it was completely impossible to focus on the movie. I reached into the box of popcorn to try to distract myself from her. She reached in at the same time, and her hand brushed against mine. Everything in me felt strangely revved up, and I was afraid I was going to throw up the Coke I'd just drunk.

I was sitting in the back of a movie theater with a girl who looked like a boy and who everyone *thought* was a boy and I was having all these weird feelings. How was this going to work?

And then she took my hand.

I spent the entire rest of the movie in a state of excitement and confusion. To this day, I don't what happened to the *Pretty in Pink* guy.

When the lights came on, she glanced at me. "Want to walk around the shopping center?"

"Sure." There was no harm in it. My parents weren't expecting me for another forty-five minutes.

She kept holding onto my hand while we made our way out of the theater and walked a block down to the strip mall. I knew that people would think she was a boy and wouldn't think twice about seeing us holding hands, but I was still a bundle of nerves. Yet I didn't want our date (was this a date? my very first date, and with a girl?) to end. When it finally did, Bri gave me a lift on her bicycle, dropping me a block from my house. Mom asked me how the movie was once I got home, and I shrugged. "I didn't really like it."

Two weeks after my next victory, at the state championships, I was still jubilant, and Bri was gracious enough to seem happy for me rather than bitter about her own loss. We celebrated together over French fries at the local diner and then hung out at her friend Mike's house on the border of our two towns. I squeezed onto the beat-up plaid couch at his house. There weren't many other places to sit, so a few guys in leather or denim jackets and girls with big hair sat on the floor around us.

Mike was passing out cans of cheap beer. I didn't want to make a big deal out of refusing, but I also didn't want to drink one. "It's cool," Mike assured me when he saw the look on my face. "You want a Coke instead?" He was a friendly guy, and I wondered what he thought about Bri bringing me. Did he know we were more than friends? That Bri liked girls? And that I liked Bri and had no idea what I was going to do about it?

I nodded, and he brought me the soda. Bri accepted a beer and murmured into my ear, "I'm just having one. Don't worry." She saw me eyeing it and offered the can to me. I took one sip just to make sure I wouldn't like it. I didn't—this *had* to be what pee tasted like.

People started disappearing from the living room in pairs. I knew they were headed into the bedrooms or maybe the bathroom to make out, and one couple even started sucking face in a corner of the living room. Bri nodded along with the music and took occasional sips of her beer, but she must have quickly sensed my discomfort because she leaned over and spoke quietly in my ear again.

"You look like you're not having too much fun. Do you want to go?"

I nodded gratefully, and after saying a quick goodbye to her friends, we headed to her place on her bike. It was about a fifteen-minute ride, and the wind in my hair felt good. Mom would kill me if she saw me on someone else's bike, and without a helmet, no less, but I was too exhilarated to worry about it just then.

"My mom's at her new boyfriend's house," Bri explained as she unlocked her front door, "so we're on our own." A shiver of excitement made its way through my spine at her words. She shrugged her jean jacket off, tossing it onto a chair whose stuffing was leaking out. There were full ashtrays on the tables that she quickly grabbed to empty into the trash. "Mom's a chain smoker," she sighed. "I hate it." So *that* was why Bri always smelled like cigarettes.

I looked at the photos on the TV stand in her living room; one was a striking black and white of a beautiful young woman holding a Typing Association of America award. "My mom was a champ," Bri explained, "until she got pregnant with me. I wasn't exactly planned."

"How old was she?"

"Nineteen. And that's her now." Bri pointed to a photo of a woman who looked like she was well into her fifties. I quickly did the math— it was hard to believe that her mom was only about thirty-five. I wasn't sure what to say.

"Come on, I'll show you around." She gestured expansively to indicate the rest of the house: a kitchen she proudly told me she herself kept sparkling clean; a dining nook; the stairs that led to the master bedroom. Finally, we were in her room tucked behind the dining nook, alone together for the very first time. She gestured for me to sit down on the edge of the bed, and took a seat lightly next to me.

I glanced mutely around the clean, sparsely furnished bedroom. Bri had a small bookshelf upon which perched a framed photo of an expensive Selectric. Her battered desk was tucked into the corner, and a couple of band posters hung near her bed. She noticed me studying one—I didn't know what else to do—and shrugged. "Motley Crue is all right, but really, I think Guns N' Roses are geniuses."

They didn't look like geniuses to me. In the poster were five long-haired, mean-looking guys in leather pants leaning against a wall.

They held liquor bottles and sported tattoos and looked like they all needed showers. But when Bri popped a cassette into her stereo, I began to understand why she liked them so much. I'd never heard anything like "Rocket Queen" before. The guitar effects were really cool, and there was something about the way the singer alternated between growling and shrilling that appealed to me. I wasn't sure what he was singing about, and I didn't know if I liked all the moaning and squealing sounds a girl was making during an instrumental. But as soon as the song ended, I was ready to hear it again.

"You should see their first video. Axl Rose, the lead singer"— Bri pointed to the redheaded bandana-wearing guy in the poster—"has on a lot of eyeliner and hairspray, and until you get to the part where he's got his shirt off, it's kind of hard to tell whether he's a boy or a girl."

That snapped me out of my music-induced reverie. I turned my focus away from the poster and onto Bri's face. There was something about her full lips that made her look like she was sulking, even when her manner was sweet and earnest, like it was right now. My stomach did a little flip-flop. She studied me. "What do you think of that?"

"I—I, uh," I stammered. "I think that's pretty cool."

Her eyes bored into me, and slowly she leaned in. I smelled cigarettes. But when her lips touched mine, they were soft and sweet; she didn't taste like smoke. She began gently nudging my lips open with her own. Where did she learn to do this stuff?! Her tongue touched mine. Was this what French kissing was all about? I wasn't sure if I liked it at first, but the longer she kissed me, the more I started to kind of melt into it. A warm stirring began to replace the somersaults my belly had been doing.

As we kissed, she began to ease me down onto the bed. "It's okay," she whispered. "I'm just going to stretch out next to you." One side of the Guns N' Roses tape ended, and the other began playing automatically. "And when you're high, you never, ever wanna come down," the singer was crooning when suddenly a woman's shrill voice pierced through Bri's bedroom door.

"Gabrielle!"

I bolted upright in the bed. Bri just froze.

"Gabrielle!" The voice was shrill, the words slurred. "What are you doing in there with the door closed?"

"Shit," Bri whispered. "My mom's home early."

She looked stricken, pale, like she'd been caught in the act—but we were fully clothed and not one hair was out of place on my head. Bri shrugged her jacket back on, like it would protect her from her shrieking mother.

"Look." Her voice was a rushed whisper. "I'm going to go out there first. Just hang out in here, don't follow me, and don't make any noise. Okay?"

I nodded.

"I'm sorry," she mouthed as she walked toward the door, closing it most of the way as she exited. It wouldn't have mattered if she *had* shut the door completely; her mother's harridan screeches could probably be heard a mile away. I cringed and shoved myself into the corner nearest Bri's closet, scrunching down as if I could become invisible if I just made myself small enough.

"What are you doing in there? What have I told you about being in your room with the door closed?"

"I'm sorry, Mom, I just—"

"I will *not* have you holed up in your room listening to that horrible, noisy music doing your disgusting dyke things and—"

"But I didn't—"

"Don't interrupt me!" A sharp crack. Her mom must have slapped her across the face, and it must have hurt.

"In your room. The door stays open or I rip it off its goddamn hinges. Do you understand?"

I heard footsteps across the living room, moving closer to Bri's room, but then her mom began climbing the steps—presumably to her own bedroom.

When I was sure the coast was clear, I crept out of Bri's room as quietly as I could.

She didn't see me at first so I whispered her name. When she glanced up, I saw tears streaking her reddened face.

"Oh my God. Are you okay?" It was a dumb question, but I didn't know what else to say.

She shook her head.

"Do you want me to wait in your room?"

"Go outside. Just… Go sit on the back porch. I'll come meet you in a minute."

I nodded and let myself out, took a seat on a broken-down lawn chair, and waited. But she never came outside.

I saw her a week later when I was leaving school. She was perched on her bike just outside of the building, her denim jacket looking as grimy as ever, dark bags under her eyes. Still, I was overjoyed at the unexpected sight of her handsome face, and I rushed toward her. My expression must have been one of pure eagerness. But I recoiled at her words. "I can't see you anymore," she blurted out, her voice hoarse as if she'd been crying. "It's complicated. I'm sorry. My mom will fucking kill me if she sees me with a pretty girl like you anywhere near my house. Or in town. Or anywhere, really."

Her eyes were downcast, like they'd been when we first met each other. "I'm a typist, for God's sake." Her voice broke. "I deserve a better life than this."

Before I could form a sentence in response, she tossed, "I have to go," over her shoulder and pedaled away.

Katie got her mom to drive us to the mall. She saw how down in the dumps I was, how heartbroken over the person she still believed to be a cute boy, and she wanted to cheer me up. After hanging out in the food court, we went to Sam Goody's to flip through records. I picked up a couple from the bands Bri told me about. They all had *so* much hair and makeup!

I was reading through a Motley Crue album's song list when a familiar guitar riff drifted out of the store's speakers. I felt a lump form in my throat immediately, and I couldn't keep my eyes from overflowing once the verses to "Sweet Child O' Mine" got underway.

Axl Rose crooned about eyes of the bluest skies. How could I not think of how Bri had commented on how beautiful she thought my blue eyes were? She had looked into those eyes and smiled at me, then kissed me. And now I might never see her again.

I hastily brushed away my tears. Caroline or one of the other girls from the team might come into the store, and I didn't want to talk about what was making me cry. I pretended to keep browsing until Katie was ready to leave.

Somehow, I had to regain my focus. I couldn't keep weeping over Bri: the national championships were coming up, and if I was going to beat the rest of the country's finest typists, I needed more than practice.

I needed a typing coach.

Naturally, I thought of Mr. F. first, but his response shocked me. He was retiring—not just from teaching, but from anything having to do with his first love: typing. "Costa Rica," he told me in a deadly serious tone. "My wife and I are going to become expatriates in a little beach town there. It's a lot cleaner than Glenwood, I'll tell you that."

Although he might have been a less-than-jovial typing coach, I had to admit that I would miss him. His understated encouragement made me feel special, because I knew how rare it was that he gave positive feedback to *anyone*. And though he didn't seem what I'd call enthusiastic—about anything, ever—I saw the way his eyes lit up when he first recognized that I might have a real talent.

"Well, goodbye, Mr. Fitz. I hope you and Mrs. Fitz get to go swimming in the ocean every day." I let him give me a stale-coffee-scented half-hug.

Now, then, to find a suitable coach. Mom and Dad said they'd match my prize money to help me pay for one. I called the Typing Association of America headquarters in New York City, where the championship battle would take place, to ask about listings for coaches in my area.

The first prospective coach I called said he didn't have availability for new clients. The second had a high-pitched, wheezing voice that I thought would quickly become unbearable. But the third one seemed like a possibility. Her name was Ms. Hinds. I'd never spoken with someone who used "Ms." instead of "Mrs." or "Miss," but I liked the idea. She said she would be able to work with me on Tuesday afternoons after school.

"Can you come by next week so we can discuss your work and set some goals?"

"Of course!" I jotted down her address, walking distance from mine.

I was surprised to see a little boy toddling around upon my arrival. "My partner will be home in about half an hour and will take care of Todd. I apologize for the distraction until then." Ms. Hinds was easy to forgive—friendly and pretty, with a kind of earthy look, she radiated warmth and confidence. I noted a picture of her with Todd and a short-haired woman. Was that who she meant by "partner"? What kind of partnership did they have?

I was shocked to see, in another photo, Todd in someone else's arms: Bri's.

"Uh—and who is that?"

"That's Todd's favorite babysitter! You know, actually, she's a competitive typist too. Her name is Bri. Maybe you know of her?"

★ ★ ★

Before I knew it, the championships were upon us. After some hesitation, I decided on my favorite pink dress again; after all, it had brought me luck last time. Trembling, my nerve endings feeling as if they were charged with electricity, I took my seat with the other contestants on the auditorium stage at the TAA headquarters in New York City. The format for this type of competition was a little different. Instead of being given printed material to retype like we did in the regionals and state championships, we had to transcribe a live reading.

I'd worked on this at home with Mom, and it wasn't my strong suit—I was more of a visual person. But I had no choice today. Ms. Hinds had rushed backstage to encourage me before I was seated alongside my competitors. "Just remember what we practiced. I'll be here the whole time," she promised.

The TAA president, Harold Saylor, would be reading a section of the Constitution aloud. He started booming into the mic, and with my heart thumping, I pounded out words—my fingers were flying. Even through my nervousness, I felt exhilarated at how speedily they were moving around, practically assuming a life of their own. I managed to tune out completely the phrases being intoned over the loudspeaker; whatever Mr. Saylor was rambling on about made no difference to me. When time was called, I folded my hands primly on my lap, eager to show that I was following the rules.

But I wasn't, not at all. Not in that championship auditorium, and certainly not outside of it.

"Ladies and gentlemen," a glamorous female TAA staff member announced into the microphone. "We ask that you remain in your seats for the next few minutes while the contestants' timings are verified. I repeat—please remain in your seats!" She looked around expectantly, as if daring anyone in the staidly-dressed audience to defy her by suddenly standing up and bolting to the exit doors. No one did.

A few murmurs among the audience, some quiet giggling among my opponents as they whispered into each other's ears and gestured furtively toward boys in the front rows. It could be any moment, now, any moment that the TAA guy would—

"Ladies and gentlemen!" Mr. Saylor stood wide-eyed. "We have an unprecedented situation here. Ms. Khrystyna Sommerville has demonstrated top speed in this competition, but"—people began to clap—"please! Hold your applause!" I saw my mother's expression instantly shift from ecstatic to crestfallen, her palms silently held an inch apart from each other.

He cleared his throat and continued. "Ms. Sommerville did not adhere to the timing regulations and has, in fact, typed something entirely different from what was dictated."

The audience issued a collective gasp. I felt my face heat up and my eyes began to prickle.

"That being said," Mr. Saylor continued, "her scores are higher than any we have previously encountered in any national championship."

Now it was my turn to gasp.

"Despite her transgression, in light of her typing speed of 115 words per minute"—and now a huge round of applause broke out and didn't stop until Mr. Saylor gestured frantically for a full thirty seconds—"I must declare Khrystyna Sommerville the TAA National Typing Champion of 1987!"

This was really happening at last. Just what I'd always wanted! Ms. Hinds hugged me and, unable to suppress a thrilled giggle as a trophy was thrust into my hands, I gazed into the audience. If only—

And then I spotted her.

Bri stood clapping and wearing the biggest grin I'd ever seen. She caught my eye and mouthed, "I love you."

I accepted my trophy, rushed off the stage, and, to my family's bewilderment, grabbed Bri's hand and led her outside of the auditorium, where I threw my arms around her and drew her to me. Just as our lips met, I heard my mother's voice: "Khrys, where are you goi—oh my!"

Bri disengaged from my arms for a moment. "What did you write?"

Should I tell her? I felt silly. Would she think it was stupid of me?

"I, uh…" I stared at the ground. "I was typing out the lyrics to 'Sweet Child O' Mine.'"

A smile spread across her face. "Really?"

"Yeah."

Bri glowed. "That's…wow."

Thank god she didn't laugh! "So, um, how's everything with you? How did you get here?"

"Ms. Hinds and her girlfriend brought me. They're letting me stay with them while my mom gets some help. I just moved my stuff in yesterday, and it's such a relief."

I'd have to explain about my new "boyfriend" to Mom later. Maybe someday she'd understand. But for now I held Bri tight, still clasping my trophy in one hand.

First Light at Dawn

Nyri Bakkalian

From: *Kate Davis*
To: *Hannah Liu*
Subject: *Re: Re: Coming out note*

Han: I'm glad you and I can get to reconnect—and to know each other for real this time. I'm totally with you, though, on needing to meet up in person, so let's plan a rendezvous in Midtown next time you're in the city. After dropping off the face of the earth like I did, I owe you a hug, an apology, dinner, and a drink. I also owe you something in the order of $280, from our epic Gettysburg road trip-pub crawl-last hurrah, way back in senior year. I swear I haven't forgotten.

But before any of that: you ask a lot of really good questions, and after all these years the least I owe you is an attempt at answering them in some reasonable fashion.

So I might as well start with the proverbial elephant in the room: the goddamn PTSD.

I think more than anything it's the unpredictability of it that I hate most of all.

Some days I'll be perfectly fine, as if nothing ever happened, I never went on that last tour, and the scars aren't even there. I start wondering if I imagined it all. On days like those, I can breathe easy and go about my day just as simply and smoothly as anyone else. I get shit done at a damn near frenetic pace and I could keep going forever, and damn, I feel limitless. I marvel at it. Is this how some people get to live *all* the time?

Other days I'll be all right, but the ghosts will be there, lingering around every corner and in the subtle shifts in the breeze. I'll be walking to work in the clear air under blue skies and the rising scent of warm asphalt and the metallic tang of gasoline will hit me and for half a second I'll be yanked out of the present by my ankles, pulled back to seven years and thousands of miles away.

Clench, unclench. Pause to breathe. Carry on as best I can. I don't want to whine, but I'm starting to feel pissed about it: it just isn't fair that I have to deal with this.

…And, boom. There comes the guilt. *Like you've got room to talk, when so many others have it worse.* But guilt or no guilt, the bad days come anyway.

On days like that, I can't take the subway in more than short hops. Something about my peripheral vision getting crowded like that just sets me off: I'll be going around like a deer in headlights, practically dragging myself one foot in front of the other from point to point until I can get into open air.

And I used to wear G-suits and fly *fighters.*

Of course if I bring it up even in passing, the first thing people ask is if I'm seeing a therapist. They're trying to be helpful, and I get that, but I'm getting tired of the suggestion. Lately I just thank them and chuckle at it. Yeah, I *am* seeing a therapist, *and* this still happens. Therapists are great, but they aren't magicians, and even under the care of the best therapist, the fact of the matter remains: trauma's a bitch.

It's the bad days I detest. The days where it feels like I'm dragging my brain through mud. There, even sleep is a battle. On the nights I can't count on dreamless oblivion, the nightmares are waiting: torn canvas and mortar holes, screams and pain and the nighttime IEDs flashing like terrible lightning against starry skies. I'm left reeling, reeling in steady horror as I stagger up the flight line. Sometimes I'm armed, sometimes I'm not, but in all of them I'm running: running breathless, pounding battered pavement and broken tarmac, running ragged and aching and alone and bleeding and unheard and God dammit, I'm in hell at al-Hakawati again and *everything hurts.* Then in an instant it'll all be gone and I'll be awake, cold sweat making me shiver against tangled sheets.

Yesterday morning was one of the bad days. I seemed to fall ass-first from nightmare into wakefulness, shaking and disoriented and sore as hell. For a moment, I think I even forgot where I was. Only the dimmest glimmer of first light at dawn filtered through the blinds. It was no comfort at all.

Come back, Skates, I silently pleaded with myself. *It's 2017,* God dammit *Skates come back. You're in bed, in New York. You're safe. The base isn't being overrun anymore. Come back.*

"Hey. Kate, honey. Hey."

It was Bree's words, still sleepy but clearer than anything in the moment, that reached me. Then a hand, hesitantly at first, alighted on my back.

You woke up your girlfriend. Way to go, dumbass.

"Hey, it's okay. I'm here."

My cheeks were wet. I was still shaking, but the tension was gone: I was a crying heap in tangled sheets. Bree pulled me gently into her waiting arms, and I didn't resist.

"I'm sorry I'm a broken mess." I sniffled. "I'm sorry."

And just like every other time I've said this, I could feel Bree gently shake her head.

"Hey. I love you," she murmured. "*All* of you."

It's the bad days I detest. But at least I don't have to face them alone.

You wanted to know how we met. It's a fair question, since Bree and I started seeing each other only *after* you and I last spoke.

Oddly enough, we first met by chance, in a café in Flushing, a long time before that damned deployment to Al-Hakawati. I wasn't out yet, obviously. And as long as I was still in the Air Force, I couldn't be. I covered my interest in things LGBT with hurried explanations: *Just an outspoken ally, I guess,* I'd say. You remember those days well.

At any rate, there was nothing more I could do, so in the meanwhile, I had to keep quiet. In the meantime, I lost myself in the minutiae of work and the different off-the-beaten-path cafés and restaurants I could find. I figured that maybe if I ignored the proverbial elephant-in-the-room that was my transness, it'd be quiet.

I took the 7 train out to Flushing and found a quiet corner in this café. And that's where I first saw Bree Wilkins: this gorgeous redhead in glasses, reading a dog-eared copy of Serrano's *Whipping Girl.* I was in the window-side couch opposite hers: people-watching and nursing a now thoroughly-cooled cup of coffee while pretending to read another tedious volume from the Chief of Staff's yearly reading list.

God, she's cute, I remember thinking, and then immediately feeling guilty for thinking it at all. Then I scolded myself. *Don't be a creep, Skates.*

She noticed I'd been staring, and threw a cursory glance at my book. "Hey, call it a librarian's idle curiosity, but what're ya reading?" A playful smirk tugged at her lips.

I shrugged at it; I'd barely cracked the spine. "Eh. Something for work." I feigned ignorance about *Whipping Girl,* but honestly, my own copy had been just as dog-eared before I'd had to get rid of it.

But Bree and I hit it off.

One "coffee date" turned to another, and then another. We were *inseparable.* We made quite the pair: the tall, closeted, trans-lady pilot and the short, redheaded librarian. I'd take the train out whenever I had leave, and we'd explore the city, compare notes on what we'd been reading, ride the subway to places neither of us had ever been.

It was glorious. I felt alive, like I hadn't in years. And eventually, there came an afternoon when I confessed the obvious.

"I think I have *feelings* for you."

We were at one of the tables in Bryant Park, underneath the trees, sparrows and pigeons nipping at the grass around our ankles. Bree turned red and looked away for a moment.

"Honestly, K.N," she said, around a relieved chuckle. "I've been feeling that way about *you* too." She reached across the table to give my hand a gentle squeeze. "Can I, um... Can I kiss you?"

We did kiss. It was a beginning.

And here we are, eight years on, through deployment and discharge and transition and the bad days: still together despite it all.

It's the little moments in our lives, the mundane stuff: I think, Han, that that's what I live for the most right now. The little everyday stuff which I would've given just about anything to have, especially during that last tour.

The *bagels*. I would've killed for an honest to god New York bagel, once, and the ride up to my favorite 24 hour deli on the Upper West Side is still damn near magical. You probably remember the place; we went there in the wee hours of that epic uptown bar crawl. The sounds, the banter, the inky odor of fresh newspapers: I'll sit there and drink it all in. Sometimes I'll sit there with my onion bagel and lox, and people watch like I did in the old days. There are some real characters up on that stretch of Amsterdam. Other times, Bree will send me up with an order, and I'll get on the South Ferry-bound 1 train and haul ass back down to Bryant Park with a shit-eatin' grin on my face and lunch for two in a big ol' brown paper bag, as I head for our lunch date.

People take bagels and lunch dates for granted.

Then there's the smell of old books. I've always loved libraries, but ever since Bree took me into the stacks at work, that first summer, there's just been *something* about that scent that calms me like little else. Obviously, it makes me think of her, but it's more than that. The archives, the stacks, the used bookstores I peruse in my off time are peaceful, even with other people around. They feel damn near sacred. Then I catch that scent of old books, even with a hint of dust, and I can feel my gut unclench. My personal demons are far, far away there. It's just me, the books, and the tangling and entangled web of words and worlds contained within their pages.

I'm actually starting to think it wouldn't be a bad idea to go get a degree and be an honest to god librarian. I can just see the memoir now—*From Ejector Seat to Reference Desk: The Kate Davis Story.*

Times have more than one way of changing us, eh, old friend?

The early mornings are probably my favorite, though. Bree and me, we don't always leave the house at the same time, so more often than not, she'll be ready for work before I am. The blinds will still be drawn, it'll still be dark out but the city's sounds will be growing steadily outside. The subway isn't far, but it's a long way into town, and she tries to head out early.

So there I'll be, barely out of bed, starting to haul my ass over to the dresser for some clothes, and Bree will already be dressed for work. She'll be standing there, silhouetted against light from the hallway, five foot four inches of attitude in a cardigan and ballet flats and a well-worn leather shoulder bag, and *God* my heart skips a beat at the sight of her. *Every. Damn. Time.*

"Headin' out," she'll say quietly. "I love you." She stands on her tiptoes and I crane my neck and God, sometimes those kisses are damn near soul-searingly amazing. And even though I'll be in barely more than my pajamas, with my hair a tangled mess, visible and invisible scars notwithstanding, the look in her eyes makes me feel like the most beautiful woman in the world.

As far as I'm concerned, though, estrogen and T-blockers had a pretty strong hand in that. Hell, they're *magical.* I know, I know, that's what you told me, way back when, but God *damn,* the stuff's incredible. I swear they took 15 years off my face. I even got carded for the first time in my life, can you believe that?

Getting *carded.* Now *that* was fucking awkward. Still awkward now, but back at the beginning?

Even the friendliest *ID please?* from the nicest bartender would already make the adrenaline kick in. I'd look left, right, cuss under my breath, and palm them my driver's license or Air Force CAC like a damn *bribe.* Most of the time, they'd just glance and hand it back. Sometimes I'd get the *squint.*

Best case scenario I'd get called by rank. "Thanks, uh…Captain." At least those times I don't technically get misgendered.

Either way, inside of about twenty seconds of interaction, my danger sense would go from zero to sixty to zero again.

Thank god my name change went through.

But then there was the first time Bree took me to a lesbian bar in the Village. The whole way down on the 1 train, I wasn't sure if it was the right thing to be doing I was second-guessing myself the entire way, until we got to through the door and up to the bar and then this old gray-haired bartender with incredibly epic tats sidled up. She eyed us over. Was she *smiling?*

"Hey gals, welcome to Straycat Blues! What'll it be?"

I looked to Bree just as she looked up at me. She gave my hand a little squeeze. *"Told ya* you'd be fine." She grinned.

Hey gals, what'll it be?

Whatever the little noise was that I made in response, it was high-pitched and ecstatic.

But there are some things that *haven't* changed.

I can *feel* a military helicopter in the pit of my stomach before I hear it with my ears.

The ones we get most often are the Coasties. They fly Jayhawks over the Hudson, especially off Battery Park, supporting the RHIB boats that run river patrol. There's a funny, comforting familiarity about it, kind of like seeing an old work friend you only ever pass in the hallway anymore. They're harmless.

Sometimes I see fast movers too: the fighters based as far out as northern New England. I'll see Vipers or Eagles or Raptors, flying training runs or turning in for CAP flights over the river.

And honestly? Those are the moments that scare me, Hannah. I look up for a moment. I wonder if I know the pilot. Occasionally, I silently critique their technique. I wince when they buzz the George Washington Bridge a little too closely. Somehow, I almost always manage to read their tail code or at least some of their colors, and I'll even smile knowingly to myself as I recognize them by squadron: one of the Deathvipers based at Barnes, or a Devil from Atlantic City.

It's all as effortless as it ever was. It's all still a part of me.

And then it happens.

For about two seconds I get wistful and I *actually wonder about going back*. The DoD's restriction on trans people ended. Assuming I passed the physical requirements, hell, I *could* do it.

But as much of a rush as it'd be, to buckle up and take a Viper up for a spin Upstate or a high-speed run down along the Jersey shore, I can't. The flying was just a tiny bright spot in something that was about eighty-five percent scars and bullshit. It wouldn't be worth it.

That chapter's closed. If it's flying I want that desperately, I can rent a fucking Cessna. After all these years, after all these miles, after all that pain, I'm *home*. I'm home, I'm whole, I'm seen.

And with all due respect to everyone who's still in? I'm not giving that up for anything.

I think, though, that the thing that bothers me the most these days about the day Al-Hakawati was overrun is that nobody ever found the orchestrator. We took out some of the insurgents on the ground but nobody ever claimed responsibility. All the resources of the US government on the case and nobody's ever figured that part of it out.

There's an air of "just because" about it, a cavalier tenor that just pisses me off.

So. I am never going to have that closure and it gets under my skin like you wouldn't believe. Sooner or later I'm gonna have to come to terms with this, but I'm not there yet.

It's funny, Han. There's a strange invincibility about flying. I mean sure, you're trained for emergencies, you go through SERE training, you get that there are emergencies we need to know how to deal with: control failure and engine failure and bird strikes and all that. But you and me, we were trained to be the top of the battlefield food chain or damn near it.

But this?

Getting overrun and watching everything burn *on the ground* isn't something I was trained for. I've only ever heard of one other squadron, a Marine unit in Afghanistan, that had this happen in recent memory.

And I think the sight of our smoldering flight line broke me. Fighters are part of a ground war but not like this: broken hulks smoldering against a night sky. Distant gunfire a running staccato.

There I was. One invisible trans woman in the ass end of nowhere in Iraq, with two rounds in her sidearm and no help in sight.

The darkness, inside and out, could've swallowed me whole.

I don't know. I feel like a failure sometimes, for breaking like that. How the hell do I explain why this has stuck with me? How do I explain why this bothers me? So many other people had it so much worse than I did.

How can I ever properly describe what I've seen?

I think it was after that moment during the Battle of Al-Hakawati that I realized I needed out. After the attack, our squadron barely had three airworthy Vipers anyway, so beyond just a token few combat missions we were preoccupied with rebuilding and rearming.

That's when I put in the paperwork. The squadron executive officer tried to talk me out of it, but even he understood, or thought he did, why I had to go.

It wasn't just what I'd seen during the battle. What he didn't understand was the other thing that happened, that moment in the dark. He *couldn't* understand it: that relieving but overwhelming feeling of clarity I'd had, standing alone and unseen in the dark in Iraq.

I remember thinking that if I'd died, there'd be all of five people in the world who would've actually seen me. And that scared me.

One way or another I needed to be seen, to be heard. And to do that, I needed to start a new chapter.

So I handed in the paperwork, and before too long, the day had come. My tour was up.

There were some things I couldn't even tell Bree over email, but I dropped hints as best I could, and told her I was getting out soon. *We have a lot to talk about when I'm back,* I said, and mostly left it at that. I thought—hoped—that she understood.

I took a transport to Rammstein, sat through bureaucratic hell for a few hours, then flew the rest of the way on a civilian flight out of Frankfurt. It was a significantly empty flight, and honestly, that was fine by me.

When I got to JFK…shit. I was so happy to see Bree I picked her up clear off the floor. We were breathless, ecstatic: when we kissed, it was like a desperate fire.

Then she leaned in and whispered the words I never knew I would've needed as desperately as I did: "Welcome home, Kate."

Home is a place. To me, home is also a person. I think that finally became clear to me, that moment in the waiting area at JFK.

Welcome home, Kate.

I was seen again. I was finally stepping out of darkness and finally into the light.

And I remember so clearly, even all these years on, how we kissed desperately, hungrily, eagerly, and how I cried in relief: the tears of a woman home again, set free at long last.

I can hardly believe it, but it's been three years now, ever since I've been on hormones. My relationship with my body can best be described as "complicated." I'm preaching to the choir, I know, but I swear, Han, there are days that it's damn maddening. My hands look too square and my jaw doesn't look right and my voice drops at all the worst times and I'm constantly on edge, always checking my six. I've had to work harder to maintain upper body strength, so now I keep as in shape as I can, keep my head clear as I can, and keep a can of mace within easy reach whenever I'm out of doors.

Maybe I'm paranoid, but I don't think so. You're only paranoid if you're wrong. And for a while this past week, I lost count of how many of us were killed, everywhere from Upstate to New Orleans and beyond. This world wants us dead, Hannah. It's kind of mind-blowing just how badly it does, too.

The way I see it? Every day I go on living is another day I've *shown* some motherfuckers.

Meanwhile, I'm getting clocked less and less these days. At least, I hope so; at any rate, most of the time I get the "ma'am" that I'm looking for. That much is good.

I've got a long way to go, but I think the important thing is that I'm still going. After everything I've been through, I'm still getting up every day and moving ahead.

I'm getting better with my voice: softening it, working the resonance out, not letting it dip too low. After two and a half years on hormones I've even got a few curves. A stranger complimented my winged eyeliner the other day. Hell, apparently I can rock an A-line dress, though I get the most inexplicable shit from older trans women for wearing a leather jacket and jump boots with it. I get exasperated eye-rolls and *you're-not-serious-about-this* finger-wagging and wholly unsolicited lectures excused with the tried and true *oh but this is for your own good, honey* excuse.

Screw 'em. This is who I am. I'm making it, one day at a time. The rough and unsatisfying bits notwithstanding, I feel more whole than I ever have.

I don't always feel beautiful, though. It'd be nice to feel that way more often, but I can't—won't—fake it. I feel okay most days, but I don't know if I'd say I feel *beautiful.*

But if you ask Bree? I've always been beautiful.

It isn't any bullshit, either. She really means it, Han. Hell, I'll be standing there doing my makeup, fretting over nothing quite going properly and my eyeliner smudging and my body just feeling like a big, scarred misshapen mess. Then Bree scoots in, to get a hairbrush or something else, and there's that hint of a husky edge to her voice.

"Hey, cutie."

I teared up, last time that happened. To have this incredible, beautiful, quirky, warm soul in my life... Damn, Han, how did I ever deserve someone like Bree?

She does damn well keeping with my ups and downs, too. Once, we were food shopping when it happened, over at one of the larger delis in Woodside. I don't quite know how to explain "it." Sometimes I hear other vets, even people like missionaries, who describe stuff like this happening after they make it home. Maybe it's got a name—I guess "reverse culture shock"? I don't know. But whatever it's called, an aisle of sliced bread will set it off.

An entire *aisle* of sliced bread, Han. I know, I know, it's mundane, but what the everloving hell? That much choice *and* that much abundance *and* everyone takes it for granted and doesn't even bat a damn eyelash at it.

So. The damn bread aisle. I dunno how long I'd been gone but suddenly Bree was right in front of me. "What's wrong, Kate? You with me?"

"Huh?"

Way to go, moron, I thought, *now she's* worried.

"You've got that look…"

I've heard the term "sensory overload" but that makes me think of someone trying to haul bricks. This is more like drowning, like there's too much of the world coming at my brain all at once. And I always feel like such a failure when it happens.

And all because of fucking *bread,* this time.

"D'you need out?"

Eyes wide, heart racing, I shook my head. I needed out but I also needed to stay right where I was, right beside her. Bree slipped her hand into mine, and we hurried into the adjoining aisle. By the time we made it to the meat counter, I was okay.

So: cold cuts, I can handle. It's the fucking bread aisle that gets me. But she's there, same as she's always been.

That reminds me: I wanted to tell you the story of how I chose my name.

So I was already out to Bree, in the weeks before that last deployment, that night. It's funny, in hindsight, how coming out played out. I went in with my heart in my throat, fully prepared to have to part ways. But she just nodded and smiled, and said she'd gotten a feeling that something of the sort was going on.

And then she said she'd been figuring out how to come out to me, too—as bi.

The timing was, apparently, perfect.

I chose my name barely a few weeks later. We were up late one night chatting idly and reading and it occurred to me suddenly.

You remember how much I hated my deadname. There's a reason why I went by my initials rather than the name itself. But for the life of me, for as long as I'd known I was trans, I never gave much thought to a better name.

Meanwhile, there I was, in another one of those annoying in-between spaces, out to myself, out to Bree, out to three or four other really close friends around town. They understood, they acknowledged it, and they kept things quiet. As far as the rest of the world was concerned, though, nothing had changed and nothing was up. The orders were finalized, the deployment was coming, and I was heading for a frontline tour at Al-Hakawati.

For the moment, though, I was okay. The deployment, the Air Force, Iraq, it was all far away, and here we were at home together in New York, reading and talking. Here I was visible. But outside?

(God, it feels weird to think of those days, of the distant sense of creeping dread, and of chafing against people's assumptions of who I was.)

I picked up the book again, thinking to pick up with reading, but the very first sentence I read stopped me cold.

She had resolved never again to belong to another than herself.

"Hey, hon?"

"Hm?" She looked up from a library copy of *Passing of the Armies.* She had her back to the sofa's opposite arm, rainbow-socked toes wiggling in my lap. "What's up?"

"I just had a thought. What if I changed the K.N.? Made it stand for Katherine Nellie." Fuck, I was feeling *inspired.*

She had resolved never again to belong to another than herself. If there was nothing else I could do, I could start with a name.

Bree set down her own book. "'Katherine Nellie Davis,'" she said slowly, with the care of someone poking their head into a newly-remade room.

"After Kate Chopin and Nellie Bly," I added quickly. Bree's suggestions had been my initial catalyst for reading a lot more nineteenth century women's words. There was something in them that resonated rather strongly for me. "Do you think it works?"

She swung her legs from my lap and scooted over to sit beside me. "What do *you* think? That's what matters most. It's *your* name."

Katherine Nellie Davis. Yes, I thought. I can make this mine. I turned to Bree and nodded. "Yeah. It works." A pause. Then, trepidation shrunk my voice to a gentle but reedy mess. "Could um… Could you call me that, around the house?"

Bree nodded. Fingers interlaced with mine, she gave my hand a gentle squeeze.

"Of course, love," she said quietly. Then, with a knowing grin, she added, "But I should ask: is it too early to say 'kiss me, Kate'?"

"You *had* to go for the easy joke, didn't you?" I laughed, but shook my head.

"Well then," she breathed, leaning in closer. "Kiss me, Kate."

We kissed. And for the first time in my life, despite the wrong set of hormones and the mid-reg haircut and the deployment to Al-Hakawati hanging over my head like a sword of Damocles, I felt beautiful.

It's taken a lot of work and a lot of hard-fought effort but I have more and more days where I feel that way. If this morning's any indicator, I think today's going to be one of the good days. I woke up rested. I just lay there and followed the ceiling plaster's whirling, hypnotic lines with my eyes.

After a while, Bree awoke, hair an unkempt red halo. She rubbed at her eyes and shifted under the rumpled covers to lean on an elbow and turn in my direction.

I murmured, "Morning, love."

"Hey, gorgeous."

We kissed good morning, and for a good long while, just held each other. Eventually, I could hear birdsong—sparrows—just outside the windowsill, and beneath it, the city rumbling and murmuring and clamoring, a thing alive.

I'm scarred, sometimes I'm a downright mess, but in all the ways that matter, I'm more whole than ever. And I'm still here, right where I belong.

"What say we get dressed," Bree suggested. "There's a new breakfast place in Flushing someone in Reference told me about the other day."

"Full circle." I smiled.

We kissed again.

I think today's going to be all right.

So I guess it comes down to this, Han. The most important thing I've learned, in this long road of healing and self-reclamation, is that the bad days happen. I can't change that any more than I could change bad flying weather. But luckily, there're good days too. Having Bree in my life, I think I'm honestly starting to believe it.

There are good days too. We just have to wait for the dawn.

My love to your family and anyone else out in Burlington who remembers me. Write back soon.

- *Kate*

Dragons Do Not

Evelyn Deshane

Juneau's dream was always the same. She was at work, underground at the mine, and they had just found the reserve of blue gems. Everyone on the team cheered so loud that it felt as if they shook the grey slate rock around them. Juneau shuddered as if she were the vibration of sound until Melody took her hand. Melody's face was framed by blonde hair made that much darker due to the lack of light. Then her hair became white as something else shone behind her, transforming her into a near-magical creature Juneau had only read about. She was so beautiful in that moment that Juneau could not help but yearn to kiss her—even in public, like this. Their faces moved together, as if drawn by a force, as if they were the only two people in the world. But soon the cheers of other workers became a ringing in Juneau's ear. Sharp, persistent, painful. All sound vacated into a piercing pinprick that shook her awake.

Muffled sound would persist until Juneau remembered she was now deaf and no longer worked in the mine. She would wake in an empty room, Melody nowhere to be found.

Juneau woke again, after the dream repeated for the second time that night. Scales brushed her palm. Keene was there, next to her. She turned on her straw mattress to see two blue-green eyes staring into hers right away.

"Hello again." Her voice felt cracked from sleep, but she couldn't tell how loud she was. Her assistant dragon nuzzled her forearm more insistently. Its blue-black scales puffed out as if it was startled.

"Don't worry," Juneau said. "It was just the dream. I'm okay. I'm fine."

When Keene still puffed out its scales, Juneau tried to be louder. "I'm awake. I'm *awake*. Don't worry. Nothing's wrong."

Juneau sat up and surveyed her room. The curtains were closed, so no light came through. But it was morning. When Keene noticed Juneau's gaze, it spread its small wings and flew to the window sill. With its teeth, it pulled back some of the curtains to let light inside. Clouds and fog blocked most of the dawn visible over Keene's spiky spine. When Juneau pulled herself to her feet and went to the window, the wind rattled the frame of the house. Orange and red leaves swirled on the ground as most of the trees surrounding her house had been stripped bare in the night.

Keene nuzzled her arm again. Its insistence had nothing to do with her nightmares, but the weather. Juneau wanted to laugh, but instead rested her palm on its head and rubbed the scales behind its ears. "I know, Keene. We'd better get moving if we want to beat the storm."

Juneau checked all her rooms before going into the kitchen. *No one there.* She knew Keene had probably already done this, and would have woken her up with more urgency if something was wrong. That was Keene's job, after all, other than to keep Juneau company.

"Keene," Juneau called as she stepped into the kitchen. "Keene?"

Keene scampered into the room and boosted itself up onto the table where its communication dominoes were. Keene's long snout tipped over the box, spilling the tiles out. Juneau knew a clatter would follow, but thanked her luck—her unfortunate luck—that she couldn't hear the mess Keene was creating.

"Well, you carry on. I'll make tea. And breakfast?"

Keene bounced on the table to communicate its joy. Juneau smiled as she worked to prepare her own small breakfast and the mouse for Keene. By the time her kettle boiled, both plates were set down on the table and Keene had completed its long domino chain. While Juneau sipped her tea and tried to decipher Keene's meaning, the dragon ate its breakfast in several quick bites, then pushed three of the last domino tablets towards her.

"Yes, yes, I know," Juneau said. "I will answer you in a bit."

The three pieces at the beginning were the standard *How are you feeling?* set with a happy face, a frowning face, and a neutral face. Each morning, Keene demanded an answer from her with those three blocks before they made their plans for the day using the others. But today, Keene was more adamant about their plan for the day—no matter how Juneau felt.

Juneau narrowed her gaze on the two cloud pieces. These dominoes were split in half, one side with a grey cloud and the other with a white one. The grey cloud connected to another grey cloud piece with a lightning bolt on the other side. A house domino stood on its own, but one with a drumstick on it (which was supposed to represent all food) was piled with several more dominos that symbolized food. Since Keene was eating happily now, Juneau knew couldn't mean it was hungry—or that she was. *The storage room?* Juneau glanced over her shoulder. She saw the doorway to her preserve area. Most of the shelves were filled; nothing had been broken into the night before by animals.

"We have enough stored away," Juneau stated. "We should be fine, Keene."

Keene shook its head. Insistent, almost angry. Using its long nose, it flipped over the box of dominos it had packed away moments earlier. More came rushing out and onto the cabin floor.

"Keene! You have to be more careful."

Juneau knelt on the ground to pick up the pieces. She hoped Keene was making conciliatory noises. She had read in the Dragon Handbook she'd first received alongside her companion animal that while dragons may not feel the exact same emotion that we call sadness, they do feel a lack of honour when they have failed in their jobs. So maybe Keene was sulking in some way. She would never hear the noises, but she appreciated any gesture of contrition. As she cleaned up, her thumb passed over a tile with a sun on it. Then another with a long coat on it, followed by a tent from a bazaar. When she placed them down on the table, Keene's eyes were as large as saucers.

"I know you're sorry," Juneau stated. "But is this what you wanted? Do you want to go to the market?"

Keene bobbed its head again. Juneau sighed. When she glanced out the windows, most of the fog and early morning greyness had subsided. Maybe things would shape up to be a nice day after all. Part of why dragons were a necessity, especially for people who were blind or hard of hearing, was because they could help predict the weather conditions. It was something about their skin and scales; Juneau couldn't remember exactly, so she consulted the handbook by her kitchen table to be sure she understood the dominos' meaning.

Dragons do not know the calendar months, but they can be trained to anticipate weather patterns. In the white-light varieties of dragon, their skin can help predict thunderstorms and protect from the worst of their effects. The blue-black dragons are sun-soakers and know when a drought is imminent. All dragons will shed scales when true winter is about to occur.

"Ah, well. That makes a lot more sense," Juneau said. Autumn was now wrapping up, which meant there would be lots of ripe and ready fruit at the market, possibly baked goods, and many more preserves to keep during the winter. It also meant it had been almost a year since the explosion in the mines which had taken her hearing. She hadn't shopped by herself in the market place in almost a year, instead relying on deliveries to her cabin as ordained by the King. As a survivor of the mining blast, the deliveries and her companion animal were large boons to her—but mere pennies to the Kingdom's wealth.

Juneau folded her arms across her chest, discarding the handbook. Keene ignored its dominos and nestled by her side. She felt the vibration of its throat, and knew the dragon was comforting her.

"So we're having a storm soon, huh? And you just want to make sure our storage of food will last? Are you sure that's all you're trying to tell me?"

Keene didn't move, only comforting her more. Juneau knew the food would last all winter, and even if she ran out, she could send a grackle to the city and they'd bring her something. The delivery service only brought necessitates, though, while the marketplace contained many beautiful things. Juneau wondered how much the marketplace had changed. Did Miss Pinkerton still have apples? Was she selling with her daughter, Abby, or had Abby finally gotten married? It had been so, so long since Juneau had left the house. So long since she'd seen anyone like Abby or Clarissa or even... Juneau didn't want to think of anyone else anymore. But she did want to go to the market. More than ever now.

"Can I even take you to the market?" Juneau wondered aloud. There were so many rules about owning a dragon—more than with any other helper animal. When Keene didn't respond to her, she picked up the Dragon Handbook again.

Dragons do not like to leave their dwellings. They are nesting creatures, determined to hoard and help. As soon as they have been assigned, they are content to stay exactly where they are.

Juneau raised an eyebrow at Keene. The dragon seemed way more willing to leave than the book gave it credit for. When Juneau's eyes scanned the pages again, they fell on the first passage of the book.

Dragons are companion animals and nothing but. Once assigned to an owner, they work like drones to a hive; dragons live to serve and have no outside motivation. They have no personal artifacts, motivations, or even names. They work, sleep, and eat. And when they sleep, they do not dream.

Juneau watched as Keene lifted itself to the kitchen window. It stuck its head outside, into the morning air, and Juneau swore the dragon smiled. It rubbed its face all along the flower garden and grasses that rose high enough to touch the sill. It seemed happier—and more eager—than Juneau had even seen. *Or maybe*, Juneau reasoned, *Keene was always like this and I never considered it because the book has told me so.* Keene was always so much more than a worker drone, devoid of name, gender, and personality. It was Keene—and Keene was always willing to help her, no matter the cost, but Keene also had things it wanted to do. She was sure of it.

"Well, Keene," Juneau said. "I think we've already broken a lot of rules. What's another one today?"

The trek to the marketplace was more difficult than Juneau thought it would be. The footpath from Juneau's cabin to the main road had been unattended for at least eight months. When she moved past the surrounding trees, she saw no signs of other houses. *I know we're supposed to be far from one another, but why can't I see anyone at all? Surely the city didn't just leave us like this?* Juneau huffed her way through some evergreens, then climbed over some rocks before she started to recognize the dirt road made from the workers' wagons.

Each time the wind blew, the air tasted like dust and minerals—just like the mines.

Juneau wondered about Melody for a moment, her best friend from when she worked in the tunnels. *More than friends, really.* Melody had kissed her when the rock salt caught on fire, the moment after they had found the blue gems under the earth. That part of her dream was always drawn from reality, as well as the white-hot bang of the explosion. Afterwards, Melody had been caught under a large rock while Juneau's ears had bled. Everyone else had been blown back from the flashpoint, injured and dying. From that point on, though, Juneau's mind got fuzzy: she had been sent to a healer and then to her cabin to recuperate, like surely other people had as well. Maybe Melody's arm would have had to be removed in order to get her out from the underground, but she was alive. Separated from her, but alive. *If I lived, she lived.* Juneau glanced behind her at the wooded area she'd travelled from. Maybe Melody was next door, and she didn't even know it, because healing cabins were too far apart and because dragons were supposed to be kept separated too. *Dragons do not take to other dragons well. They must be kept bonded to their masters at all times.* That was why she hadn't seen Melody. A rule about dragons.

Or maybe… Just like in Juneau's nightmares, Melody really was gone.

Keene nuzzled her from inside her shoulder bag. Juneau touched under its throat, felt the hum of conciliatory noises, and then turned her attention back towards the marketplace.

"Shhh," she said. "We're almost here."

Keene probably made a grumbling noise before it went back inside. Keene wasn't a big dragon, but it was deceptively heavy. *It has to be the scales. It's armoured like one of the King's Men.* When Juneau almost tripped over a rock, Keene was jostled in her bag. The dragon poked its head outside the opening. It had no eyebrows, but Juneau swore its scales were furrowed.

"What? I'm trying to walk. There are lots of rocks."

Keene shook its head then disappeared inside again. Juneau was caught off guard for a moment when she saw a wagon filled to the brim with wood and white rocks. The wagon moved silently in front of her, pausing before a large fence that led to the city centre.

"We're here," she whispered.

Keene nudged her through the bag. *Go forward,* its prod communicated.

Juneau took a step, but soon stopped. "How will I communicate with the sellers?"

Juneau could read lips, but she knew she had to pass as a "normal" speaker in order to not raise suspicions. People didn't like to be reminded of the mine explosion, so having her around would prove difficult. *Which was why dragons weren't allowed here.* It wasn't that dragons didn't like to leave home; that had been an embellished lie the handbook printed in order to discourage owners from bringing them. Dragons meant a disability, which meant a casualty that the city could not prevent. *What else have I been lied to about?*

"We should go back," Juneau huffed. "I don't want to be here."

Keene prodded her again. The sharp edges of its scales brushed through the tote bag. Not mean, not painful, but persistent. It seemed to say *no*, again and again. *Go forward.*

When another wagon went by, this time filled with old pots and pans covered with a waxy residue, the old man on the back glanced at Juneau.

"Hello," his lips seemed to say.

Juneau tried to smile and took a step forward. Then another. It was easier as she reached the gate and the cobblestone surface of the marketplace. Maybe she couldn't talk to anyone, but she could go inside, look around, and then go home again. Something fun for an afternoon. That was it.

People swarmed together in blobs of bright colours and iridescent light. Two aisles of vendors were set up by the city fountain near the apothecary shop. At least, Juneau thought it was the apothecary. Her memory of the place was almost a year old. More buildings had been erected beside the small shack, making architecture spill outwards from the dense city centre. There was now another butcher's shop filled with lamb and goat, and a spice vendor with dried leaves hanging on the outside, along with men in red and blue tents selling copper goods and other metals. Juneau kept her eyes peeled on the signs, reading and committing the new information to memory. When people glanced at her or waved at her, she merely nodded.

For the most part, no one saw her. In a crowd, like inside the tunnels of the mines, she became invisible. Her heart ached for Melody at that moment.

"I miss her," she said aloud. "So much more than I thought."

No one reacted to Juneau's utterance. *Maybe I'm not loud enough?* She wondered if she had been whispering with Keene all this time in the cabin.

When Keene jerked her bag to the side, Juneau allowed the dragon to lead the way. Keene stopped fidgeting when she stopped by a table full of jewelry, run by an elderly woman with olive skin. Juneau's attention went right to the silver chains.

"Hello," Juneau said carefully. She watched the saleslady to be sure she was properly heard.

The old woman nodded, then spoke something too quickly for Juneau to catch. Her heart thundered. "Pardon me?"

The woman repeated what she had said, then gestured towards a blue necklace. A blue gem. Juneau forgot her worry, and was taken in by the jewel. *I used to mine this. This is Zaffrite, the gem of the*

Agateland. She touched the edge, feeling for a price tag. She saw the numbers just as the woman stated it aloud.

"Seven stones for a beautiful stone," the woman said slowly. "Would you like to try it on?"

Juneau shook her head. Seven stone was the allowance she got for her cabin in one year. There was no way they were selling the exact item that took her hearing for so much. And she got so little. Juneau put the jewelry piece back carefully before she became too worked up. The woman tried to say something else to Juneau, but Juneau turned away.

"Sorry," she mumbled. But it didn't do much. She knew that. She rushed away from the table so quickly Juneau didn't see the person she bumped into.

"Excuse me!" the person shouted. *Yelled.* Juneau could feel the vibrations from his body. A flat chest covered with a soft fabric in a light red, almost pink, colour.

Juneau took a step back as she fumbled her apologies. Her bag fell off her shoulder and onto the ground in her efforts. Keene's head peaked out, and Juneau gasped. The man she had bumped into—at least, Juneau thought he was a man—followed Juneau's gaze to the ground. Juneau saw his own bag on the ground, and a similar snout peeking out of it.

"You?" Juneau asked. "You have a—"

"Shhh." The man put a finger to his lips. He reached down to grab his own bag when his white-light dragon ran out. To Juneau's surprise, Keene scrambled out of her shoulder bag and took off after the white-light dragon. Both of them disappeared behind the apothecary's cabin.

"Oh no!" she cried.

The man's face was turned away from her, so she couldn't hear or see his own cries. The man's long brown hair was held behind back in a ponytail and he wore a dress down to his knees that was spotted with crude flower drawings. Silver braces were attached to his forearms and extended down as crutches. Each step he took forward was done first by the silver crutches on his arms, then by his legs.

"Are you...?" Juneau said aloud, only to realize he wasn't paying attention to her. He was already steadily moving towards the corner where their dragons had disappeared. Juneau had no choice but to follow.

Around the corner, Keene and the other dragon chased one another's tails. Juneau could tell right away it was in jest, not in anger or retribution. She recognized the gleam in Keene's eyes and the toothy grin on its face. When the white-light dragon caught its tail, tugging on it, Keene's scales lifted up like it was happy.

"Aww," Juneau said. "This is sweet."

The stranger said something. Juneau tapped his arm, careful not to get in the way of his crutches.

"I'm deaf," she said. "Can you say that again while facing me? So I can read your lips?"

The man formed an O with his mouth. "You're like me?"

Juneau didn't answer. She wasn't sure what he meant. When the silence became too much, Juneau said, "I have a dragon from the Agateland Council. Because of the mining explosion."

The man nodded. "I'm a water reserve casualty."

Juneau didn't know what that meant. She didn't have a chance to ask. The man glanced around them, attentive to the swelling crowds of the marketplace. "We need to hide our dragons."

Juneau crouched down to see Keene. She wanted to call Keene by name, but instead held open her bag and ushered the dragon inside with her hand movements. The man's dragon scaled up his canes and moved inside his dress, just around his chest. Juneau could see the dragon's eye peek out from the button line of the dress, but its gaze merely looked like a marble.

"Is that why you wear a dress?" she asked. "To hide your dragon?"

"I'm a woman. That's why I wear a dress."

"Oh." Juneau blushed. She really had thought she was dealing with a man. Or perhaps a monk who wore special clothing Juneau knew nothing about. "I didn't know... I'm sorry."

"It's all right. Everyone's allowed a mistake," the woman said slowly. "My name is Anna. My dragon is Deirdre."

"Hello, Anna. I'm Juneau." Juneau made sure to pronounce the syllables in her name carefully. "You named your dragon too?"

"Yes, of course! Everyone deserves a good name. She picked it, too."

"Your dragon picked a name?"

Anna nodded and repeated her next words twice to be sure Juneau could make them out. "My dragon picked *her* name. Her pronouns, too. She and I are quite alike."

"I'm not sure what you mean."

"We are both women though the Agateland Council says otherwise."

Juneau was quiet for a long time, trying to process this. Both of their dragons were tucked away, so she wasn't worried about bystanders seeing them. Juneau was slightly worried about Anna's canes, though, and what people would do if they saw her outside her house. Did Anna get a house like Juneau did, or was that just for the mining explosion? What exactly was the water reserve and why did that mean Anna needed to walk with forearm braces and a tremble to her steps? Did the water reserve also cause her femininity?

"I'm not sure what any of this means," Juneau confessed. "The Dragon Handbook says dragons are drones. And drones have no personal motivations. They don't even dream."

"And yet you named your dragon."

"Well, yes. But after an adjective. It was so keen to do everything for me at first, I just thought…"

"You just thought that you were right. Something deep down told you so."

After a moment, Juneau nodded.

"Exactly. People break rules not because they're bad but because they know something else is right. And your dragon's definitely not a drone—not like they say, anyway. She's much more than that."

"She?" Juneau repeated. Keene rustled in the bag, scales up. Excited. "Why do you say she?"

Anna shrugged. "I suppose I see a lot of similarities between Keene and Deirdre. Could be nothing, or it could be an insight. Sort of like…"

"Takes one to know one?" Juneau suggested as a chill went through her. Those were the exact words Melody had used to explain how she'd known Juneau was special. In an underground working environment, where people barely knew each other's first names, the two had found one another and known they were different. There was no logic to it, only a sense of belonging more intense than anything she'd ever felt before.

Anna smiled. "I suppose so. I see myself in Deirdre, and in a way, Keene, too. But then again, you could always ask to be sure. Asking is the only way we ever really know."

"Um. Yes. Sure." Juneau nodded and shook off the rest of her reverie with another glance at her dragon. "I suppose Keene is more than what the handbook says. And I could ask."

"Good. Does Keene like the name?"

"Um. I don't know. I'm still learning, I suppose. But I'll ask. I promise."

Anna nodded. She reached out a finger and held it near the side of Keene's head as Keene peeked out of the bag. "Can I?"

"Sure. You can pet Keene."

Anna did so, rubbing her hands around the ears. Juneau could feel the vibrations of Keene's pleasant noises. Though Deirdre stayed tucked tightly inside Anna's dress, Juneau spotted her wide eyes through the button holes. She was just as happy, too.

"You know the dominos?" Anna said.

"Yeah. The King's Advisors give us each a set."

"They do, but there are more. The set they give you covers the basics of daily life and care. But you can get another set from the market and Keene can tell you all sorts of things. I got more dominos for Deirdre and I realized she had her own name, other than the one I had given her."

"Oh. What was it—her name before?"

"Doesn't matter," Anna said. "I also learned a lot about the city, communicating like this."

"Really? More than just the weather?"

"Yes." Anna's eyes flitted around, assessing the people passing by. "I don't think we can talk very much here. I have to go. They're already mad I left the house."

"Oh, of course. Sorry."

"Juneau." Anna touched Juneau's arm to get her attention. "Be careful on your way home. Do not stay out too long."

This was a friendly warning; nothing like the Dragon Handbook's bold font. Juneau swallowed, and then nodded. "Thank you, Anna."

"No problem at all." Anna tapped the dragon inside her dress before she added, "You know, they can dream too. Just like us. And we should be paying far more attention to that."

Anna turned away before Juneau could respond—not that she really knew what to say. The language of dreams still made her feel cold inside. It reminded her of the blue gems that matched Melody's eyes and the sickening sound of the blast. It made her feel hollow, like those few seconds of consciousness before fully waking up and Keene taking over for the day: a deeply alert sense of awareness which allowed her to fully remember the day she lost her hearing. Melody was stuck, her arm gone—but the light of her face was also gone, too. Juneau didn't need to hear to understand the signs of death, no more than she needed to sleep to understand her dreams. Melody was gone, no coming back. Juneau was the only survivor of the mine blast, which had been why she was sanctioned off into the woods. Her exile had been far more than making sure the council didn't look bad in the face of an explosion; it was making sure that there was no evidence of the explosion at all. If all they had to hide was Juneau, then the rest of the world could move on.

But I'm not the only accident survivor. There was a water reserve, and that had causalities, too. Only when Juneau realized that she wasn't actually alone in her trauma had Melody's death been able to sink in.

Keene poked his outside the bag and nuzzled Juneau. She quickly wiped a tear away and tried to smile down at it. *Or her?* So many things had changed in that moment—maybe Keene was one of them, too.

Juneau found the domino booth two minutes later. Now that she knew what she was looking for, everything seemed too obvious. A woman with long curls sat in front of a cloth sign with *Divination Station* painted in gold and purple. Several rows of stone dominos lined one side of the display, followed by tarot cards, playing cards, small hands with lines etched on the palm, and several other areas filled with many coloured stones. A customer in green clothing examined a deck of cards in front of the saleslady, leaving the domino display empty. Juneau approached with caution—but also excitement.

Everything seemed to be categorized by theme. Juneau spotted the set she and Keene used all the time as the Broken Bone Collection. What did that even mean? Juneau turned away. The Moon Chime collection contained bone-white dominos that were delicately painted with phases of the moon, stars, and other sky-items she didn't know the name for. The Flower Helper set contained many different flowers in just as many colours, with brown dominos for dirt, green ones for grass, and carefully painted seedlings. The Crossing Afterlife collection contained several dominos with skulls, crossbones, tombstones, and fire—all rendered with an ominous colour palette full of dark maroon, purples, and greys that all seemed to resemble shades of bruises.

The woman knocked on the table in front of Juneau, causing her to start. When Juneau glanced up, she tried not to give herself away.

"Hello, young lady," the woman greeted. "What can I get for you?"

"I don't know yet," Juneau carefully articulated.

"Do you know what you want to see?"

"Pardon me?"

"You're a querent when you're here. The future is for those who want to look."

Juneau smiled awkwardly. She had no idea what a querent was, or if she'd even rendered the word correctly in her mind. She went over all the phonemes she could think of, before giving up. When the man examining the cards demanded the woman's attention again, Juneau let out a sigh.

Juneau glanced down at the new sets. When she came across the set marked as Querent Questions, she realized she'd heard the woman correctly. But what was a querent? The dominos in this set displayed images of a flame, wax in water, tea cups, and a hand with an eye in the centre of it. Juneau furrowed her brows as Keene rustled in her bag.

"Let me know," she whispered. "Let me know what you need."

When Juneau crossed by the flower set again, Keene nearly vibrated in agreement.

"This one?" Juneau picked up the dominos. They were heavier than her own; definitely made from better quality stone. Keene vibrated again, and Juneau smiled.

"Young lady?" The woman appeared in front of Juneau. "Have you decided?"

"Yes, I'd like these." Juneau's gaze fell back along the other sets, where she also picked up the querent deck. "And these."

"Excellent choice."

The woman took both sets of dominos from Juneau and wrapped them in cloth. Juneau pulled out the small amount of coin she had left and exchanged it for her purchase. She slipped the dominos into the bag with her dragon, careful not to let anyone see. In a matter of a few seconds, the whole ordeal was done.

"We did it," Juneau murmured. Each step she took was filled with a new type of bounce and urgency. She scanned the courtyard for Anna and Deirdre, but they were nowhere to be seen. Her heart panged with a familiar sense of loss—but also possibility.

Keene nuzzled Juneau's elbow when she reached the edge of the courtyard, now out of the line of sight. The dragon continued to nuzzle her, its scales up. She couldn't tell if it was as excited as her, or worried.

"I know, I know." A chill wind blew by and struck Juneau deep down in her bones. "Do not worry, my dragon. We are going home."

✦✦✦

Juneau felt the rumble of thunder and the prick of rain on her skin long before she stepped inside her small cabin. She stumbled towards her straw mattress and collapsed right away. Keene slipped out of the bag, spreading its tiny wings as it opened his mouth to let out cries Juneau couldn't hear, but she hoped they were the pleasant murmurings of being home. She reached out to touch Keene's back and then rubbed her fingers over its ears.

"Hey there," she said. "I think we took on a bit too much today. I need to rest."

Keene flew over to the window and tugged on the curtains. Juneau felt the low thudding of rain on the roof. No snow yet, but she knew that'd be soon. Once the window was closed, Keene perched on the sill with its head down. *Ashamed?* Juneau wondered. She was half-tempted to look through her Dragon Handbook to see what this emotion was supposed to be, but the idea didn't excite her anymore. *Dragons do not feel sadness, only duty,* she remembered. But it was wrong. Dragons, like humans, dream and know far, far more than anyone in power says they do.

"Come here, you. I think we have things to do." Juneau emptied her tote bag onto her mattress, scattering some of the dominos on the floor. Keene gave a few excited cries before it rushed over and started picking up the fallen dominos. Juneau realized the dragon was communicating with her, not merely cleaning, when its message was complete. A rose and a happy face were laid out in front of her.

"You want a rose?"

Keene shook its head. It went through a couple more versions of the same message, adding a seedling, and then taking away the happy face. Adding a few blank ones, before taking them away. It even cracked into the querent set, which had several letter clusters, before Juneau held her hands over the messages.

"How about I ask and you answer? That seems to be the easiest. So. Are you a boy or a girl?"

Keene waggled its tail to knock around some of the dominos. She watched with wide eyes as Keene spelled out GRL.

"A girl?" Juneau asked. "Are you a girl?"

Keene bobbed its—*her*—head into a nod. After the first elation of understanding, Juneau felt a pang of guilt. She was mistaking everyone. *How come I didn't know sooner?* Juneau chastised herself, then ceased. There was never a reason to ask the question before. But they were talking now. They were doing so many things now.

"What do you want me to call you, if you're a girl?" Juneau asked.

The dragon wagged her tail excitedly. She nudged the same titles as before. *A happy face and a rose. A happy face and a rose.* Juneau repeated the option until her mind seemed to unearth the answer, like finding a gem underground. "Oh. You don't want a rose. You want to be Rose."

The dragon's large eyes seemed to water over, as if with tears, even if Juneau knew that was impossible. *Or was it?* No, these were tears. Happy tears. Juneau knew that now.

"Rose," Juneau said, smiling. "I think I have it now. Your name is Rose."

Rose's scales went up, before she scampered over to Juneau's lap. She circled the soft spots on Juneau's folded legs for a good resting place, something she had done lots of time before, but Juneau was suddenly moved by the action. *Rose. Rose. She's a sweetheart. My sweetheart.* Juneau smiled as she patted over the scales and her spine.

A flash of lightning flickered through the curtains before Juneau felt the roll of thunder. She glanced at the querent pieces from the other set as darkness rolled over the cabin. There were so many more questions Juneau wanted to ask, but the rain made her tired and the cooler air made her knees ache.

"You're not going anywhere, are you?" Juneau asked Rose playfully as she settled down into bed. "Because now that we can really talk, I want to tell you so many things."

Rose nuzzled Juneau's chin, then attempted to pull the blankets up to cover Juneau more. "So many things, like about Melody," Juneau added, her voice trembling a bit. "Because even if she's gone, she still happened. And maybe if I tell someone, it won't hurt as much. And maybe… I can dream about something else. Someone else."

Anna's face flashed in Juneau's mind. Her long hair, her dress, and even her crutches seemed so much more beautiful than before. So much more magical.

"And maybe," Juneau added, "after a while, you can tell me more things about you."

Rose made another noise, something Juneau could only feel through the scales. There would be time, Juneau knew, *so* much time to figure out what dragons really did do. For now, she and Rose fell asleep, and dreamed of something more.

Planchette

Carolyn Gage

Dedicated to Kathleen Carbone

~ Trigger warning for references to sexual assault and violence ~

Cast of Characters
JUDE: A female teen with masculine gender presentation, 14.
MOLLIE: A female teen with feminine gender presentation, 14.
REVEREND LEHEE: A large, traditionally masculine man, 40's.

Scene
Mollie's bedroom, upstairs in a middle-class, Victorian house in Portsmouth, New Hampshire. The bedroom is on the ocean. The first "nor'easter" of the season is raging.

Time
Early fall, 1879.

Lights come up on a girl's upstairs bedroom. The room is in a turret of a Queen Anne Victorian house in Portsmouth, New Hampshire. The windows of the bedroom face the ocean. It is an early October evening in 1879. There is a nor'easter rising outside the windows. A fourteen-year old girl enters. This is MOLLIE. She wears the clothing typical of a middle-class, New England schoolgirl.

MOLLIE: *(Exasperated, she turns and calls behind her.)* It's up here... *(Pause. She turns toward the door.)* Judith...? *(Louder.)*

Judith…! Are you coming? My bedroom is up *here*! *(JUDE enters, also fourteen. JUDE wears boys' clothing and carries a large Gladstone bag. JUDE, has had an eye on MOLLIE for a while, identifying her as another loner, but MOLLIE's hostility was not something JUDE expected and JUDE has had to readjust expectations.)*

JUDE: *(Surly.)* "Jude." My name is "Jude."

MOLLIE: Well, everyone in school calls you "Judith."

JUDE: They're wrong.

MOLLIE: Your *grandparents* call you "Judith."

JUDE: Yeah, and I never even met them until a month ago. So I think I know my own name better than they do. It's "Jude." *(She dumps the bag and crosses to the windows.)*

MOLLIE: *(Uncomfortable.)* Well, I don't care what your name is. It wasn't my idea for you to spend the night, so you're just going to have to entertain yourself.

JUDE: *(Angry.)* If you didn't want me to stay over, then why did you invite me?

MOLLIE: Because my father told me I had to.

JUDE: Why is that any of his funeral?

MOLLIE: Your grandparents go to our church, and they told him they were going to Dover for the night, but they didn't want you staying by yourself while they were gone.

JUDE: Yeah, well, I'm used to it.

MOLLIE: They said you didn't have any friends.

JUDE: I've got lots of friends back in Denver! I've only been in Portsmouth for a month. What about *you*?

MOLLIE: I have friends.

JUDE: No, you don't. I see you in school. Nobody ever talks to you.

MOLLIE: *(Stung.)* Actually, I prefer my own company. *(She opens her book and starts to read. The sound of rising wind. JUDE crosses to the window.)*

JUDE: Big storm... A real gully-washer.

MOLLIE: *(Not looking up.)* It's called a nor'easter.

JUDE: *(Another pause.)* If this was my room, I'd haul that bed over here, so I could stay up and watch the ocean all night.

MOLLIE: *(Not looking up.)* I grew up on an island. I've seen the ocean.

JUDE: *(Staring out the window.)* Out in Denver, water's scarce as hen's teeth. Hardly even any lakes. Instead of ocean, we got a hundred miles of prairie.

MOLLIE: *(Not looking up.)* Denver sounds pretty dry and ugly.

JUDE: *(Looking pointedly at her.)* Plenty of dry and ugly right here in New Hampshire. *(MOLLIE looks up and JUDE turns back to the window.)* You may have seen the ocean, but I bet you haven't seen the elephant.

MOLLIE: *(Back to her book.)* Yes, I have. At the circus.

JUDE: You've seen *an* elephant, but you haven't seen *the* elephant.

MOLLIE: *(Not looking up.)* I don't know what you're talking about.

JUDE: It's a saying we have in the Territories.

MOLLIE: *(Not looking up.)* There's no elephants in the West. *(Another crack of thunder. JUDE turns back to the window, pulls a flask out of a pocket, and takes a swig.)*

MOLLIE: *(Glancing up, alarmed.)* What's that?

JUDE: "Old Orchard..." *(MOLLIE does not understand the slang.)* Whiskey. *(Offering it to her.)*

MOLLIE: You can't drink that here!

JUDE: I could drink whenever I wanted in Denver. My daddy used to take me in the saloons with him. Told everyone I was his son.

MOLLIE: Well, *my* father's a minister, and he doesn't allow spirits in the house.

JUDE: *(Tucking the flask back in the jacket, JUDE mutters.)* New Hampshire...

MOLLIE: If you liked it so much in Denver, why didn't you stay there?

JUDE: Oh, believe me, I wanted to. If our house hadn't burned down, I'd still be there.

MOLLIE: Your house burned down? *(A crack of thunder.)*

JUDE: Isn't that what I just said? *(MOLLIE waits. JUDE turns away.)* Prairie fire. That's how my mother died. *(She pauses. MOLLIE looks shocked.)* My pa wanted me to stay in Denver with him, but her parents got all worked up about it... made him put me on the train back East. He didn't want to... *(Pause.)* My pa's goin' to send for me as soon as he gets settled.

MOLLIE: *(Long pause.)* I'm sorry about your mother. *(JUDE doesn't say anything, but takes out the flask again.)* You still can't drink here.

JUDE: *(Exploding.)* Folks can't do *nothing* in Portsmouth! Whole town so high-falutin' they got nothing better to do than tell other people how to live! Out in the Territories, nobody's got time to worry about what anybody else is doing.

MOLLIE: Nobody tells me what to do in Portsmouth.

JUDE: That's because you're already doing everything like you're supposed to.

MOLLIE: What do you mean?

JUDE: Clothes. Take clothes. Out there, it's the frontier. Everybody's doing everybody's work. People just wear what they feel like and nobody cares. And Denver's full of saloons and brothels. I've been to both.

MOLLIE: I wouldn't brag about that.

JUDE: Why? Nobody cares. Nobody goes to church in Denver.

MOLLIE: I don't believe that.

JUDE: Yeah, well, go see for yourself. After you've seen the elephant, not much point in praying.

MOLLIE: *(Exasperated.)* Okay, what does that mean?

JUDE: It's hard to explain to someone like you… from the East.

MOLLIE: Well, try.

JUDE: *(Long sigh. MOLLIE waits.)* Folks go west to see something they've never seen before, something they can't tame… something wild, bigger than life, busting out with magnificence… something there aren't any words for, so they say they're going to see the elephant. And then they pack up everything in a wagon and they head out. But then there's these storms on the plains… hailstones as big as bricks, and there's flooding and prairie fires and fever… bad roads and no grass… The wagon wheels bust, the cattle die, the babies die… Folks run out of food; then they run out of water... And that's when they know they've seen the elephant. You can't never forget it once you've seen it, and you can't describe it neither. You've seen it or you haven't. *(MOLLIE becomes very quiet and JUDE takes out the flask again. This time MOLLIE does not stop her. JUDE watches the ocean. Thunder.)* You used to live out there? *(MOLLIE nods.)* Can you see your island from here... I mean in the daytime?

MOLLIE: No. And it's a *group* of islands... the Isles of Shoals. They're ten miles out.

JUDE: *(Musing.)* I was ten miles outside of Denver.

MOLLIE: It was like another world. When someone had to come to Portsmouth for supplies, we would say they were going to the continent.

JUDE: *(A laugh.)* "Going to the continent..." I like that. You know what we say about traveling back East...? "We're going to the 'land of steady habits.'" *(MOLLIE laughs for the first time. Thunder. JUDE turns back to the window.)* Must have been something to be on an island during a storm like this.

MOLLIE: I liked it.

JUDE: You weren't scared?

MOLLIE: No. *(Pause.)* I was scared when it was calm.

JUDE: How come?

MOLLIE: When the sea is calm, people can land on your island. *(Louder thunder. MOLLIE looks away. Another silence. JUDE watches the storm.)*

JUDE: That tree's gonna blow down tonight.

MOLLIE: No, it's not. It's a hundred years old.

JUDE: *(Deafening crack of thunder.)* What was the name of your island?

MOLLIE: Londoner's. There's a map on the wall. *(She points to it. JUDE crosses to the map.)* There were nine of them… Londoner's, Appledore, Star, Seavey, Malaga, Cedar, White, and Duck Island.

JUDE: *(Studying the map.)* And Smuttynose. You forgot one. *(MOLLIE doesn't say anything.)* Is that a joke?

MOLLIE: *(Quietly.)* The fishermen named it… Because of the way it looked with seaweed all over one end of it. *(JUDE is laughing.)*

JUDE: Don't you think that's funny? "Snotnose Island?" *(MOLLIE has picked up her book and is reading. Loud thunder. JUDE looks out the window again. Another pause.)* What are you reading?

MOLLIE: *(Not looking up.)* Eight Cousins. By Louisa May Alcott.

JUDE: What's it about?

MOLLIE: *(After a pause.)* It's about this orphan girl Rose, who goes to live with her great aunts. And they're all rich, and they try to dress her up and teach her manners, but then her guardian uncle comes back, and she goes to live with him and his seven boys... You'd like the uncle. He tells Rose that girls shouldn't wear bustles and corsets.

JUDE: *(Bristling.)* Why would that matter to me? *(Surprised, MOLLIE looks at her.)* I don't care what girls wear.

MOLLIE: Then how come you're wearing boys' clothes?

JUDE: *(Looking out the window.)* Ever hear of a hobdehoy? *(Turning to MOLLIE.)* Yeah, well, a hobdehoy is someone that everyone thinks is a girl, but when they grow up, they're men. *(She turns back to the window. Loud thunder. MOLLIE is speechless.)* I read a lot, too. Ever hear of Ned Buntline?

MOLLIE: No...

JUDE: Everybody reads him out West... Old Ned is some pumpkins... One time he got in this duel with a man who thought he was after his wife—which he wasn't, but it was a duel, so Ned had to kill him. Shot him right between the eyes, but then the man's brother was standing there, and *he* pulled out his gun and started shooting at Ned... So then Ned ran into this hotel and tried to hide, but there were so many people looking for him, he didn't have a chance... So he had to jump off a balcony, but the balcony was dang near fifty feet high, so he got pretty busted up from the fall, and that's the only reason they caught him. So then they took him down to the jail, because it was still daylight, but as soon as the sun went down, they came back—about a hundred of them—and they broke into the jail and dragged him out of the cell and down the street. It was going to

be what we call a "necktie party," but Ned was trying to stall them…
So first he asked them to go fetch him a minister, but they wouldn't
do that, so then he started asking if they would just shoot him, but
they wouldn't do that either, because they were all fired up for a
hanging… So then they put the rope around his neck and hauled him
up on an awning post, and he was sure enough starting to die but just
then the rope broke—or maybe somebody cut it—but by then they
figured Ned was so near gone they might as well take him back to
the jail… and so that's what they did, only Ned didn't die… and they
ended up letting him go, because it was a duel and he had shot the
man fair and square. And after that, he went and got himself married
seven different times and he wrote hundreds of stories… and I've
read them all.

MOLLIE: That sounds like one of them.

JUDE: In New Hampshire maybe… but out in the Territories
things like that happen all the time. Which is why I'm going back
there. *(Thunder.)*

MOLLIE: *(Closing her book.)* You know what I think? I think
everybody in Denver drinks too much and tells tall stories. *(JUDE
shrugs.)* There's no elephants in Colorado… and there's no such
thing as a hobdehoy!

JUDE: Yes, there is.

MOLLIE: No, there isn't.

JUDE: Yeah, there is.

MOLLIE: Prove it. Take off your shirt.

JUDE: Why would I do that?

MOLLIE: Because I think you're a girl.

JUDE: I don't care what you think. *(Thunder.)*

MOLLIE: I happen to know for a fact you're a liar. Your mother didn't die in a fire. *(JUDE looks at her.)* Your grandparents came over here to talk to my father, because he's their minister, and I heard them say that your mother had gone crazy and that they had to go out to Denver to get her and bring her back and put her in the asylum in Dover, because your father had abandoned her… and they said that *you* were in the Denver Orphan's Home! *(JUDE looks at her in silence, turns and picks up the Gladstone bag.)* Where are you going? *(JUDE exits. MOLLIE calls out.)* Wait! Where are you going..? *(Tremendous thunder.)* There's a storm…! *(MOLLIE runs out the door leaving the stage empty for a moment. We hear her calling JUDE's name from offstage.) Jude..! Jude…! (Running back in, MOLLIE crosses to the window, throws open the window, and leans out. The sound of the wind is very loud.)* Jude…! *Jude…* ! *(JUDE has re-entered the room quietly and comes up behind MOLLIE, making a sudden gesture of pushing her out the window. MOLLIE screams and shoves JUDE. She begins to hit JUDE. She continues to scream. It's clear that she is having some kind of post-traumatic episode. JUDE is terrified.)*

JUDE: Whoa…! Whoa! It's just me… Mollie, stop! Mollie…! *(JUDE closes the window. MOLLIE is shaking and panting.)* It was just a dang *joke*…!

MOLLIE: *Not funny*! *(MOLLIE, hyperventilating, won't look at her. JUDE, at a loss, suddenly remembers something.)*

JUDE: Hey, Mollie... I forgot... I brought you something! *(MOLLIE is lost in her pain. JUDE opens the Gladstone bag and takes out a heart-shaped wooden item.)* Yeah. Made it myself out in Denver. See? *(MOLLIE doesn't look up.)* Yeah. Well... It's called "planchette." It's a parlor game. *(JUDE crosses over to MOLLIE and puts planchette into MOLLIE's hands.)* See...? It's got two little wheels, and you put a pencil in the hole here. Wait a minute... *(JUDE crosses back to the Gladstone bag to retrieve a pencil.)* It goes like this... *(Putting the pencil into the hole.)* There. Now... I need a piece of paper... *(Long silence. MOLLIE points toward the desk. JUDE retrieves the paper and places it under the planchette.)* There!

MOLLIE: How does it work?

JUDE: Well... I'll show you. You put *your* hand *here*... Lightly... Like this... *(JUDE models.)* And I have *my* hand *here*. And then one of us asks a question. *(Thunder.)*

MOLLIE: And then what?

JUDE: Well... then planchette starts to move, and the pencil will spell out the answer. *(MOLLIE pulls back her hands abruptly.)* What?

MOLLIE: This is about communicating with spirits.

JUDE: *(Bosh.)* No, it's not... People just pretend that it's ghosts, but it's really just themselves.

MOLLIE: Then what's the point?

JUDE: It's a game. *(Pause.)* Gets things going when people run out of things to say. *(Long pause. Slowly MOLLIE puts her hand back on planchette.)*

MOLLIE: Well, ask something.

JUDE: "What color are Mollie's eyes?" *(They both stare at the platform. Slowly it begins to move.)*

MOLLIE: You're pushing it.

JUDE: No, I'm not.

MOLLIE: You have to be.

JUDE: I don't feel like I'm pushing it.

MOLLIE: You're lying.

JUDE: No, I'm not. Look... "B"...

MOLLIE: *(Looking.)* "Blue." That's too easy.

JUDE: Then you ask something.

MOLLIE: Anything?

JUDE: Yeah. *(MOLLIE looks at JUDE closely. Distant thunder. The storm has begun to move off.)*

MOLLIE: *(Slowly and deliberately, staring into JUDE's eyes.)* "Does Jude have breasts?" *(JUDE, unflinching, meets MOLLIE's gaze. They have a staring contest. Slowly, planchette begins to move. Neither looks down.)* It's moving…

JUDE: *(The two are both still staring.)* I know.

MOLLIE: Don't you want to look?

JUDE: Don't you? It's your question. *(MOLLIE looks down, but JUDE doesn't.)* My turn. *(Never taking her eyes off MOLLIE's.)* "What is Mollie so afraid of?" *(Another long stalemate. Slowly the board moves. JUDE looks down.)* "L." *(Pause.)* "O." *(Pause)* "V…"

MOLLIE: *(Interrupting.)* It's not a "v!" *(Without looking.)* It's a "u."

JUDE: L-o-u…. "I." *(Pause.)* "S." L-o-u-i-s. Louis. *(JUDE looks up.)* Who's Louis?

MOLLIE: If you lived here, you wouldn't have to ask.

JUDE: Who is he?

MOLLIE: Louis Wagner.

JUDE: Are you going to tell me who he is?

MOLLIE: No.

JUDE: *(JUDE looks at her.)* You know, I *could* leave. I can get back into my grandparents' house through the coal chute. The only reason I came back was because I didn't want *you* to get in trouble… *(MOLLIE doesn't say anything.)* Okay. *(JUDE crosses toward the Gladstone bag.)*

MOLLIE: Wait! *(JUDE turns. MOLLIE rises and crosses to the wall. Distant thunder. She takes down the map and sets it on the floor by the planchette, pointing to one of the islands.)* This one is Londoner's Island… *(JUDE looks at her for a moment before dropping the bag and crossing to her. The two crouch together over the map.)* We were the only family on the island. And here's Smuttynose… The one you think is so funny.

JUDE: I said I thought the *name* was funny.

MOLLIE: There were two Norwegian women on Smuttynose… Maren and Anethe. My mother used to row me over there to visit, and sometimes, if she had to go to Portsmouth—

JUDE: To the continent—

MOLLIE: … to the continent, she would leave me with Maren and Anethe for the day. Their husbands were fishermen, so they were gone most of the time. Maren and Anethe had the whole island to themselves. *(She pauses.)*

JUDE: What were they like?

MOLLIE: Well… They spoke Norwegian a lot. And they were very proud of their little house. They had some china from Norway… and they had plants in the house. They loved their dishes… and they were so happy. That's what I remember. People on the islands complained a lot... about the weather, and about the fishing... It was not easy to live on the Isles of Shoals, but they always seemed so happy. I used to beg my mother to take me over to Smuttynose. It was a fairytale island to me, and because they didn't have any children, they would always make a fuss over me, and I loved it. Anethe had this long, blond hair— so long, she could sit on it—and she used to let me comb it out and braid it. She would hold me on her lap and teach me Norwegian songs... *(Pause.)* I remember one time I asked Maren if Anethe was an angel. I had heard my father talking about them in his sermons, and I was curious. Anethe was laughing at me, but Maren got very serious, and she said, "Yes, Mollie, it is true. Anethe is an angel that God has sent to me." *(MOLLIE falls silent. JUDE reaches out and touches her hand. MOLLIE pulls her hand away as if it had been burned.)*

JUDE: And Louis?

MOLLIE: Louis was a Prussian fisherman. He worked with their husbands... He didn't have a wife or a home. He just boarded in Portsmouth when he wasn't out on the boats. But one spring he got sick, and because he didn't have any money or anyone to take care of him, Maren and Anethe's husbands told him he could stay with them on Smuttynose, until he could work again. I remember Louis was there for a long time... the whole summer. We all thought he was faking, just so Maren and Anethe would take care of him. Maren really hated him. She would always speak Norwegian in front of him, and he would get so mad. And then he would try to get back at her by speaking to her in German, but she didn't care, because nobody wanted to hear what he had to say anyway. All he did was brag about his girlfriends... One time Louis came over to Londoners, and he started talking to my father about hell... He said he would rather be a devil than an angel, because angels have nothing but pretty hair and wings, but the devil has power. He said that twice, "Power."

JUDE: What did your father say?

MOLLIE: He was too shocked to say anything, but he told me later that he thought Louis had a past that "would not bear inspection." *(A long silence. JUDE gets up abruptly and crosses to the Gladstone bag.)* Where are you going?

JUDE: I brought us some doin's... soda biscuits and marmalade, in case we got hungry. *(JUDE unwraps the biscuits and opens a tin of marmalade. MOLLIE watches in silence.)* Made them myself...

MOLLIE: You cook?

JUDE: Somebody had to. *(Spreading the marmalade on a biscuit.)* Not the marmalade... but I made the biscuits... There. *(Handing it to MOLLIE.)* See if you like it... I could hire on as a cook in a hotel if I wanted to, but I've got a better plan. Want to hear it? *(MOLLIE nods. While she eats, JUDE talks.)* When I get back to Denver, I'm going to save up my money to buy me a field camera, and then I'm going to set up a studio and make portraits of people, because people are always wanting to send pictures back East... You know—when they get married or have babies. *(Smiling.)* But, see, that way, *they'll* be the ones fussin' about what to wear, and *I'll* be the one doing the staring. *And* I figure I can take pictures of the mountains and make postcards and sell them. Denver's on the plain, but you can still see the Rocky Mountains, with the snow and the sunsets... A lot bigger than the hills you got here. You ought to come out and see them... *(MOLLIE freezes.)* Or maybe I'll send you one of my postcards...

(There's a long pause. JUDE quizzically pushes the planchette in her direction.)

MOLLIE: You want me to finish the story...

JUDE: Do you want to finish it? *(MOLLIE puts the biscuit down. JUDE waits while MOLLIE brushes the crumbs off her fingers. After a moment, she resumes her story.)*

MOLLIE: One night in March, Louis was on the docks in Portsmouth, and he saw Anethe and Maren's husbands, who were waiting for a trainload of bait from Boston. The train was late and they told him they were going to be there all night. So then, Louis knew the women would be alone on the island. So he stole a dory and rowed out to Smuttynose.

JUDE: He rowed ten miles at night?

MOLLIE: It was a clear night and the tide was with him. And he could see the lighthouse on White Island.

JUDE: How long ago was this?

MOLLIE: Six years.

JUDE: So you were seven?

MOLLIE: Eight. *(JUDE nods.)*

JUDE: ... so he rowed out...

MOLLIE: He rowed out. And then he went to the house... And Maren's sister was staying with them, but Louis didn't know that. She was sleeping in the kitchen and when she heard him come in, she started screaming and woke up Anethe and Maren... And Louis started beating Maren's sister over the head with a chair, and then Maren opened the bedroom door and managed to drag her into the room, but while she was doing this, Louis started smashing *her* over the head... but she still managed to get her sister into the bedroom and hold the door closed against Louis... She was really strong. *(JUDE nods.)* So while she's holding the door she turns and tells Anethe to climb out the window—

JUDE: Wait... They were in the same room?

MOLLIE: They always slept together when the men were away. So Anethe opened the window and climbed out, and Maren told her to yell over to Star Island for help, but Anethe was too scared. So then Maren told her to run, but Anethe said she couldn't. And Louis must have figured out what was going on, because he let go of the door and ran outside and around the house to where Anethe was standing in the snow. And when she saw him, all she could do was keep saying his name, over and over: "Louis! Louis! Louis!" And then he killed her with an axe from the woodpile. And Maren saw the whole thing from the window.

JUDE: That must have been terrible.

MOLLIE: And then Louis saw Maren and turned to run back in the house, so he could kill her, but as soon as he was around the corner, Maren jumped out of the window—

JUDE: What about her sister?

MOLLIE: It was too late to save her... *(Pause.)* And the whole time, Maren's little dog Ringe kept barking and barking. Maren said that Ringe's barking saved her life, because at first she was going to run down to one of the fish shacks and hide, but because Ringe was making so much noise, she knew Louis would find her. So she picked up Ringe and ran with him across the island, and they hid under a big rock that was right next to the shore, so the sound of the waves would drown out the barking. But Maren told me that she held his little mouth closed all night anyway. And Louis would have found her if she had gone to the fish shack, because the next day, they saw his footprints going around and around the outside of it.

JUDE: So he left?

MOLLIE: He rowed back to Portsmouth. And in the morning Maren was able to shout over to Appledore, and someone came and got her. And Celia Thaxter, who owned the hotel on Appledore... she took care of her.

JUDE: And what about Louis?

MOLLIE: They arrested him in Boston. And then, three years ago they finally hanged him. But he told everyone that he was innocent. He said Maren did it, and there are people who believed him.

JUDE: And you were only eight. Were you scared?

MOLLIE: Everyone was scared. *(JUDE doesn't say anything.)* But the worst was when my mother took me over to Appledore to visit Maren. She was completely different. She didn't even look the same. It was like she was dead while she was still alive. That scared me more than anything.

JUDE: *(Nodding.)* I've seen that. *(Pause.)* Out West.

MOLLIE: She went back to Norway, but her husband stayed in Portsmouth. *(JUDE nods.)* There's something else I didn't tell you— *(There is a sudden loud knock on the door. MOLLIE jumps, and JUDE stands up.)*

REV. LEHEE: *(Offstage.)* Mollie…? *(Knocking.)*

MOLLIE: *(To JUDE.)* It's my father.

REV. LEHEE: *(Offstage.)* Mollie…? *(MOLLIE crosses to the door and opens it. REVEREND LEHEE is a gentle giant of a man. Dressed in middle-class clothing, he cuts an imposing, paternal figure.)*

MOLLIE: Father…?

REV. LEHEE: Sorry to interrupt you girls… *(Turning to JUDE.)* Hello, Judith… *(Turning back to MOLLIE.)* I heard that tree in the front blow down… *(JUDE shoots a look at MOLLIE. MOLLIE looks away.)* … and I wanted to come up here and survey the damage. *(He crosses to the window. MOLLIE and JUDE follow him.)* Well, it missed the house, but it's blocking the street.

JUDE: *(Eager for his approval.)* I can help you buck the tree, sir. *(REV. LEHEE turns to JUDE.)* I used to cut our firewood in Denver.

REV. LEHEE: *(Laying a hand on JUDE's shoulder, he speaks indulgently.)* Well, I think that's going to be a job for the menfolk… I'll ask your grandfather to give me a hand. *(MOLLIE looks down.*

Her father notices this and turns to her.) Bucking and hauling wood is dangerous work. I'm surprised Judith's parents let her do it.

JUDE: My pa taught me to build, too. So I could take care of my mother.

REV. LEHEE: *(Smiling gently at JUDE.)* That's a *husband's* job... taking care of the women.

MOLLIE: What if a woman doesn't have a husband?

REV. LEHEE: *(To MOLLIE.)* Then the men of her family will care for her.

JUDE: What if they die?

REV. LEHEE: *(To JUDE.)* Then the men of the church will step in. *(JUDE looks down.)* Judith, I understand from your grandfather that you weren't raised in the church, and I was sorry to hear that.

JUDE: I don't mind.

REV. LEHEE: Life can be pretty tough without the Lord to guide us. *(Turning to MOLLIE.)* Isn't that right? *(To both of them.)* God knows a lot more than we do... He sees the road ahead, as *well* as the road behind. And that's why He's given us rules... so we don't get lost or take any wrong turns. But we have to follow His rules. *(Turning abruptly to MOLLIE.)* Moll, honey, I want you to pick out a couple of your dresses to give to Judith. *(MOLLIE is shocked and becomes progressively more mortified by her father's lack of sensitivity.)*

JUDE: *(Alarmed.)* Oh, that's okay, Reverend Lehee. I don't need them.

REV. LEHEE: Looks to me like you do.

JUDE: My grandparents said I could wear what I want.

REV. LEHEE: *(Smiling gently.)* They told me they really want you to start wearing dresses.

JUDE: But they said—

REV. LEHEE: *(Cutting her off.)* I *know* what they said, but, Judith, put yourself in their shoes. They feel like their only daughter was taken away from them, and now they are terrified of losing their only granddaughter. I can't believe that a girl as sensitive as yourself would want to keep doing something that is causing them so much pain, after everything they've been through.

JUDE: *(Frustrated.)* But what I wear doesn't have anything to do with them…!

REV. LEHEE: *(Gently cutting her off.)* Stop… Judith. Do you know what Deuteronomy is? *(Silence.)* It's the fifth book of the Holy Bible. And it contains the word of God that he gave to Moses, to lead his people out of the wilderness. It's the rules, Judith. The rules we were talking about. *(He quotes.)* *"The woman shall not wear that which pertaineth unto a man, neither shall a man put on a woman's garment: for all that do so are abomination unto the Lord thy God."* *(He puts a hand on JUDE's shoulder again.)* Now, I want you to tell me that you'll wear the dresses that Mollie gives you. *(Long silence.*

JUDE looks away.) All right. *(REVEREND LEHEE turns to his daughter.)* Mollie, don't let her go home without them. *(A long sigh. The Reverend exits. JUDE is fighting tears of rage and humiliation.)*

MOLLIE: I'm sorry, Jude.

JUDE: *(Exploding in fury.)* It's an abomination to wear a *dress*! How would he like it if someone told him *he* had to wear one? *(JUDE begins to cry with rage during this rant.)* Men taking care of women? *(Pacing.)* My pa went off to Denver and left us in that… *shack*! … For weeks—sometimes a whole month! Just me and her… And if it hadn't been for me bucking wood and doing all the cooking, we would have frozen and starved to death! She couldn't do *anything*… just sit there and talk to herself and cry all day. And then she tried to burn down the house… *nine times*! *(Sobbing and nearly incoherent.)* She tried to burn it down *nine times… with us in it*! I couldn't let her alone for a minute… I had to stay up at night, watching her… What was I supposed to do? Tie my mother up like an animal…? *What was I supposed to do?* But sometimes I just couldn't keep awake, no matter how much coffee I drank. So one night last summer, I fell asleep and she did it. She lit a fire in every room. When I woke up, the whole house was on fire, and there she was… standing there in her nightgown, laughing. If it hadn't been for me, she would have burned up! She didn't care. She didn't care if I died, either. She was just standing there laughing. Wouldn't even help me pump water, when I was running back and forth, working my legs off trying to put it out… By morning, it was all burned up. Everything we owned. Burned to cinders… *(JUDE is crying.)* And then folks said it was my fault. They said I should have done something. What was I supposed to do? *What the hell was I supposed to do? (JUDE is sobbing. MOLLIE doesn't say anything. After a minute, she picks up the planchette, and sets it between them. She places her fingers on it, waiting for JUDE.)* What?

MOLLIE: You ask.

JUDE: *(Shaking her head.)* I can't think of anything.

MOLLIE: Nothing? *(JUDE pushes planchette gently away, rises, and crosses to the window. MOLLIE watches.)* Jude, I didn't finish the story... *(Pause.)* Those two women... Maren and Anethe... they were sweethearts.

JUDE: *(Without turning.)* I figured they were.

MOLLIE: That's why Louis came back to kill them.

JUDE: Yeah. I figured that, too.

MOLLIE: After he killed Anethe, he dragged her body back into the house, and they found her body with the nightgown pushed up. *(Long silence. JUDE nods.)*

MOLLIE: He couldn't stand how happy they were with each other... without the men. I don't think anybody knew they were sweethearts except Louis and me, because we were the only ones who ever saw them on their island together like that.

JUDE: That's a big secret for an eight-year-old.

MOLLIE: You knew that women could be like that?

JUDE: Yeah. I've seen them in Denver. *(Pause.)* And sometimes people just *think* it's two women, but one of them is really a man. *(JUDE turns and looks at MOLLIE. MOLLIE looks away. Suddenly, JUDE crosses to planchette.)* I want to ask a question. *JUDE sits, fingers on the wood. Tentatively, MOLLIE joins JUDE.)*

MOLLIE: Well…?

JUDE: *(Asking the board.)* What is Mollie so afraid of?

MOLLIE: You already asked that.

JUDE: Yeah, but Louis is dead. *(Again to the board.)* "What is Mollie so afraid of?"

MOLLIE: *(Starting to rise.)* This is stupid.

JUDE: *(With a hand on her wrist.)* Wait. *(MOLLIE puts her hands back on planchette. A long pause.)* It's not moving.

MOLLIE: I know.

JUDE: You're holding it down! *(Angry.)* That's not fair…

MOLLIE: *(Quickly.)* I'm like Maren and Anethe. *(She gets up abruptly and crosses to the window. JUDE watches her. There's a long silence.)*

JUDE: Storm's startin' to pass. *(MOLLIE does not respond.)* I take it back.

MOLLIE: *(Not turning.)* What?

JUDE: What I said about you not seeing the elephant. *(Long silence.)*

MOLLIE: Do you know where in Denver you're going to build your photography studio?

JUDE: Not going to build it.

MOLLIE: *(Turning.)* But you said—

JUDE: I'm going to lease me a room over a dry goods store on Larimer Street. *(Pause.)* Larimer Street is in the middle of Denver, right next to this creek... Cherry Creek... I'll show you. *(JUDE takes the pencil out of planchette and begins to draw a map. MOLLIE crosses to watch.)* The creek runs clear through the city. Like this... here... Here's 14th Street, and Larimer crosses it, like this... and here's Cherry Creek... And my studio's going to be right up here... I'll be able to see Cherry Creek from the window... *(Still drawing.)* I figure I'll sleep in the studio first few years... easier just to have the whole thing all on one stick... *(JUDE looks up.)* There actually ain't no cherries on "Cherry Creek." They named it that on account of the *choke*cherries, and you can't eat them. They're so sour they make your mouth all puckered... *(MOLLIE smiles and JUDE takes her hand gently.)* And there's beavers in the creek. They build their dams outside of Denver, but then they come back downstream to eat. You can see them swimming... And there's trout and perch. I can just step outside my studio and go fishing for my dinner... Got crayfish there, too... And here's the Rockies... *(JUDE draws them.)*... to the west... You look right across Cherry Creek and you can see them. Mollie, you got to see the Rockies... *(A tense pause. This is a proposal.)*

MOLLIE: I'd like to. *(JUDE relaxes. Lights begin to fade.)*

JUDE: And at night, the moon comes up right over them, like it was a lantern—sometimes so bright you could read your book by them... That's the truth.

Blackout

End of Play

Birthday Landscapes

E H Timms

As Cavallan opened the cottage door, there was a shriek of "Da!" and the twins pounded across the main room and skidded to a halt in front of him, practically vibrating with excitement. "You made it!"

"As you see." He shifted on his crutches, easing his arms through the straps of his pack. He set the pack down beside the door, shedding fame and legends along with it until he was only Val. Having propped his sword against the pack, he headed for the central table and its benches. Emlan and Lusi orbited him like eager moons as he moved, never quite touching. Once he sat down, they bounced up to sit on either side of him. He clamped his mental shields down as tightly as he could and gave each of them a quick sideways hug. At almost eight, they knew that was the most touch he was able to give them, and they drew back nearly as fast as he did. Emlan hugged his knees and beamed up at Val as Lusi chattered non-stop about how great it was to have Da there for their birthday, and how he was only just in time, and had he brought anything, and could they have apples in their birthday porridge, just this once?

He deferred the question of the porridge to their mother, Rose, with a lift of his eyebrow.

She considered it for a moment, then conceded with a nod. "If," she added, "you go to bed soon, and stay there. No peeking."

Emlan shot off the bench and was halfway up the loft ladder before Lusi caught up with him. They looked back, and Val raised his hand in a gesture between a salute and a wave. Twin grins flared back like sunshine, and the pair vanished up through the hatch.

Rose chuckled, swung a kettle full of water over the hearth to heat, and lifted a pair of mugs down from the shelf. "Apples it is, then." She picked up a jar of herbal tea mix and spooned dried leaves into both mugs, before setting that jar down and picking up another. "One scoop or two?"

"Two. It was a long ride."

She nodded and added two spoonsful of painkiller to Val's mug. Once the water was hot, she filled the mugs and brought them to the table, along with a plate of bread and cheese, and three winter-stored apples.

Val blew on his tea and sipped. The sharpness of the mint didn't quite hide the bitterness of the painkiller, but it came close. He reached for an apple. "I can peel these while you check on the little ones, if you like?"

"Deal."

Val stifled a chuckle with another mouthful of bitter tea as Rose followed the twins up the ladder. She had said exactly the same thing in that tone when they'd finalised their business arrangement for children. She'd wanted children without the pressure to perform in bed, and had been happy to bring them up alone if necessary. He'd been neutral, not expecting to live long enough to see them grow, and not wanting to land someone else with unwanted work. Early negotiations had been awkward, until they had both realised that the other was aromantic, and bonded again in the laughter caused by assumptions. Neither of them wanted the pain of trying to explain to someone deeply in love that their hearts worked...differently. Matched orientations meant they didn't have to explain. Instead, they were friends, colleagues in the job of bringing the children up, and he'd agreed to stay as long as life allowed. The apple peel slid free under the pressure of his knife, curling like his smile. That laughter hadn't been the first thing they bonded over, of course. That had been over archery, of all the things that might bring a warrior and a weaver together. Later discussions over the details had cleared out a good few other misunderstandings before they ever became major problems. Now he had good companionship, a home that welcomed him, and no lopsided alloro love to cause problems on either side. They hadn't expected twins, but the kids were growing up well, and if he didn't come back the next time he was called off to the war— well, he didn't. This time he had, so he would lay the worries to one side for the birthday party tomorrow. Not because they weren't real, or valid, but because there was no point mentioning what would spoil the kids' enjoyment. He reached the end of the apple, laid apple and peel side by side, rubbed a hand over his knee, chewed his way through a slice of bread, and took up the second apple. He had half the peel off that one when Rose came back down and took a seat opposite him.

She said, "They're all but asleep now. I think they'll be fine." She drew her own belt knife, picked up the peeled apple, cut it into quarters, and began to trim out the core. "You made good time on the road."

He nodded. "I hoped to be back in time, but I couldn't be sure until I actually arrived. Then I had to settle Dav in the guild stables and rinse off the travel dirt before I could come up here." He shifted his weight absently on the bench to ease a spike of pain and took the last of the peel off the apple with a flourish.

"And that'd take a bit, as fussy as that new horse of yours is. And you did send word you'd arrived, luckily, or they'd already have gone up to bed." Rose's grin brightened her eyes and deepened the folds at the corners of them as she teased gently.

"Well, I'd have had to be a birthday gift to them, wouldn't I? Only without the wrapping paper. Still, I'm here, and they know it. They'll have to make do with cloak pins." He nodded in the general direction of his pack, laid down apple and peel, and picked up the third apple.

Rose finished coring the first apple and started on the second. "Are you up to sleeping in the house tonight, or should I go and make up the bed in the Nook?"

Val thought about it, kneading his leg. The Nook was built at the far end of the yard, where he wouldn't have to worry about being heard or about power leaking out through his dreams. It was tempting, but he eventually shook his head. "I should be all right in here, I think. But thanks."

"If you say so." Rose looked sceptical at his qualifier, and bent over the apples, chopping them briskly.

Val hastily recalled the third apple lying idle in his hands and resumed peeling it. Once done, he passed it over and watched her dark gold fingers flex as she quartered, cored, and chopped it. "Archery practice on tomorrow?"

"Yes. Are you joining me and the twins?"

"I hope so, but I'd better see how I am in the morning."

Rose nodded and tossed the chopped apple into a pot, along with the porridge oats. She added water, covered the top, and set it on the edge of the banked fire. Val collected his crutches, eased himself off the bench, and went to unpack. He hung his sword up on the weapons rack, tossed the filthy travel gear into a basket ready for laundering, and finally took the deflated remainder of the pack through to the ground floor bedroom. The cloak pins went in the tiny lock-box, along with his own silvery circlet. He folded the banner carefully into the bottom of his storage chest and tossed the empty pack in after it. A shadow crossed the floor, and he looked up to see Rose leaning on the door frame.

She asked, "Done?"

He nodded, with a quick smile that deepened all the weary lines around his eyes.

She nodded back. "I'll go blow the candles out, you get some sleep," she said, and vanished back into the other room.

Val sighed, pulled off the thin leather band pinning his hair down against his head, and ran his fingers through the now-free hair. Shedding boots, clothes and foot, he unwound the magical brace around his knee long enough to clean and check the scars beneath. He replaced the brace at its softest setting, shrugged into an old shirt, and rolled into his bed to lie with his back to the wall. He fell asleep before Rose returned to take her place in the other bed.

★★★

He stood alone behind a wall on the Vakkar mountain pass, blades in his hands, rigid brace on his leg, and the invading army flowing up the pass towards him. A whispered command and light poured from the silvery circlet to coat him like a second skin. The snarl of a wolfhound rippled from his mouth and echoed off the stones, but there was no one to back him up, and no end to the army and in the end...

No.

He was standing at the wall across the pass, with Jake grinning beside him, when Mak sauntered up to take over the watch duty. They paused a moment, ducking into the shelter of the wall whenever the catapult stones and flagons hurtled towards them. Then Val started back to the cook fire. He didn't see the flagon full of pitch until too late and it burst, covering all three of them and...

No.

He was sitting on horseback, on a flat muddy plain, watching the swirl of a battle and trying to read how it was going. Trying to spot when and where the reserves he led could make a crucial difference, and just waiting and waiting, as the battle went on and on, and swirled closer and closer, and the king's banner—his blood brother's banner—went down, and...

★★★

A soft woollen ball bounced off his head, and his hands slashed up in an instinctive defensive reaction before he slammed far enough out of sleep to recognise where he was.

"You're leaking," Rose informed him with a yawn. By the sound of it, she was safely on the far side of the room. "The wall again?"

He did nothing but breathe for a moment, then reached down with a shaky hand and tossed the ball back towards Rose. "Thanks." He imagined shields closing in around his core like a metal-petaled flower, and pulled the equally-shielded blanket up over his head to prevent any more inadvertent projections. Perhaps the Nook would have been better after all, but he didn't want to come to rely on it.

Breathe, he told himself. *You cope with this in an army camp beside the battlefield, you can do it here. Breathe.* He tried to follow his own instructions but it built only a fragile semblance of calm. Beneath that, he could feel the shake in his breath, in his muscles, in the frantic shudder of his heart. He shifted on the bed, stretched out each leg in turn, flexed his toes, rolled his ankle, ran his right thumb up and down the sides of his index finger, tasted salt on his lips, and closed his eyes once more. The woollen blanket cradled his skin in scratchy fibres. Rose had woven the blanket. He recognised the pattern she preferred. The wall against his back provided an illusion of safety; his body instinctively fitting itself into a place he could more easily defend. Even here, in his own home, even where his mind thought it was safe, those instincts couldn't be denied. You could take the warrior away from the war, but you couldn't, once you'd been there, take the war out of the warrior. He consciously steadied his breath into a sleep pattern and slowed the spinning of his mind by mentally running through dagger drills, starting with the simplest and gradually getting more complicated. Somewhere between the ninth and tenth drill, he dropped off again.

✦ ✦ ✦

"Da?" a voice whispered.

"Emlan?" Val opened his eyes and folded back the blanket.

Emlan danced beside his bed. The light showed the grey of pre-dawn. "Da! Are you going to be with us all day?"

"On your birthday? I certainly hope so!" Val sat up cautiously, waiting to see which muscles were going to protest today, and swung his legs off the bed. Once he'd cleared the end of the bed, Emlan climbed up to sit there, bare feet tucked under the blanket, while Val attached his prosthetic foot, adjusted his brace, and dressed in clean but worn clothes. "Come on," he told his son, "let's go and have tea."

They went out together, quiet except for the pad of Emlan's feet and the tap of Val's crutches on the stone floor. Val stirred the fire into life. Emlan filled the kettle. They each fetched their own mug, working around each other with the ease of long practice.

"Got a preference, kid?"

Emlan nodded. "Mint, please!"

"All right, two mint coming up." Val tucked his crutches close, and added mint to both mugs, followed by a scoop of painkiller in his own. Once the water boiled, he used a cloth to pick the kettle up and filled the mugs. Emlan hopped up on a stool to stir them, then carried both mugs very carefully to the table. He and Val slid onto the same bench and cradled their mugs.

Val touched his mug to Emlan's. "Happy birthday, Emlan." They drank together: not speaking, just sitting with each other.

The quiet ended when Lusi stuck her sleepy face out of the hatch. She waved at them and clattered down the ladder with her boots slung around her neck. She waved off an offer of tea with a grimace that turned into a yawn and slumped onto the other bench.

Val grinned crookedly. "Happy birthday, Lusi."

She flapped a hand in response and dropped her boots to the floor so she could stuff her feet into them.

Rose emerged in clothes just as clean and worn as Val's, looking wide awake. "Shoes, Emlan, please."

Emlan gulped the last of his tea and scuttled off to get his shoes. When he slid back down the ladder again, Val got up, rinsed out the cups, and set them aside, before turning towards the door.

They arrived at the Warrior's guild as a group, but Emlan and Lusi promptly ran off to join the trainees with whom they practised archery. They were the youngest there, but not the worst. Val watched them for a moment. For once, the twins looked alike in dust-coloured breeches, beige shirts, scuffed boots, brown skin, and black hair. They even wore equally serious expressions. He stored this memory beside the others he had of them and joined Rose at the adult range. There was a stool waiting there for him, which he sighed over—someone at the guild had clearly spotted his return and knew him far too well—then took out of practicality. Val accepted a bow and a ground quiver of arrows, wedged one end into the instep of his flesh foot, and strung the bow with a smooth steadiness. The feel of a weapon in his hand anchored him in the here and now, and he dropped into the cool balm of a practice session. It was simple. It was repetitive. It was safe, and steadying, and the one thing he was any good at: the one constant running through his life. Lift and nock and draw and shoot, over and over, while the arrows marched inward across the target. He was almost sorry when the session came to an end, but he traded the bow for his crutches again and made his way across to the stables to check on Dav. He and the horse were a match in so many ways: not just in their bay colouring, but in determination and endurance as well. The stall smelled of hay, clean straw, and clean horse, and Dav's mane and tail had been freshly brushed, so Val gave him only a pat on the neck and left him to rest after yesterday's hard ride.

Rose was waiting when he came out, but the twins had run on ahead. They fell in side by side as they walked home along the dirt road, and the children came back to circle them and dart off again like eager birds around a berry bush. He grinned at Rose. "They do seem to take after you, bird-lady," he told her, teasing her with the old nickname. She'd come to the masked midsummer dance as a bird one year, the first year they'd talked in any depth. He'd gone as the famous hero Cavallan, the King's Hound, disguising himself as—himself.

"Well, hero," she quipped back, "since they got your looks, it's only fair that they got something from me as well."

Back home, they ate apple-laden porridge, decorated with apple peel that had been fried with honey. For long minutes, there was only the sound of spoon scraping against bowl and bowl scraping against table. Val finished first, and went to get his gifts. He'd give them a gift of his time as well but the pins would give them something solid to remember by if—when—he didn't come back someday.

He handed out the tiny parcels. Emlan unwrapped his slowly, picking open the knot in the string and unfolding the scrap of paper one layer at a time. He cradled the round pewter disk engraved with tiny dogs against his chest and whispered, "Thank you."

Lusi tore into hers, pulling at the string until it loosened enough to slide off in a tangle of half-knotted strands and plucking her disk free of the remains of the paper. She took one look at the tiny engraved birds and squealed, "I love it!"

Val smiled. "All right, kids, it's your birthday. I'm at your disposal. Either take turns, or decide together what you want to do."

Lusi pulled Emlan into a corner to whisper. Rose and Val took the opportunity to clear the table and clean up, even as the twins' heated murmurs of argument, punctuated with glances at Val, resolved into Lusi darting up the ladder into the loft. She came sliding down a few minutes later, with the chalk pouch clutched tight, and rejoined Emlan. They clasped hands and approached Val together.

"We want landscapes, please, Da," Lusi proclaimed, and held out the chalk she had fetched.

"Very well," Val replied. He nudged a chair up to the end of the table and took the chalk pouch. "What kind of landscape do you want to start with?" He sat down and fished out one of the pieces of chalk.

"Plains," Emlan piped up. "With grass and flowers, not all mud and sand and stone!"

Lusi scowled. "I wanted hills. Can I have them second?"

"Of course." Val breathed slowly and gathered himself, then racked his memory until a suitable plains landscape came to mind. He visualised it, took up the chalk, and sketched it out in map form on the table. He ran his finger around the edge of the map to mark a boundary, then fed out a trickle of power. The map flowed upward into a miniature illusion of the real landscape, and the twins bounded up to flank him at the table.

Emlan folded his arms on the table and propped his chin on his hands with a sigh of happiness. "Horses," he requested. "Horses just as horses, having fun!"

"Horses it is." Val popped a herd of horses into the middle of the plains and set them to kicking up their heels and running for the joy of running. Drawn from memories of his own horses, he watched his old mounts appear among the herd. "Right," he said, his finger hovering over one of the racing horses. "This is Breeze, he loves to run and hates being caught by anyone. He's incredibly good at dodging and evading…" *Cavallan summons and rides the wind*, ran the stories told by the bards, ever and always catching only a little of reality and turning it over until they got something they could like and believe was real. They'd heard him yelling for Breeze, wretched animal that wouldn't come to be caught or to be ridden, and now they insisted that it was the wind, always the wind. And of course, it was the bard's version that went ahead of him, and that everyone believed, not the truth of the matter. "And this is Silver," he went on aloud, pointing out a small but sturdy grey draft horse. "She's not anywhere near as fast as Breeze, but she's strong and she's clever about finding her way. She looks after people, especially younglings and foals, and tries to keep them safely out of danger…" Silver had looked after him when he was a toddler tagging along behind his father's mercenary company. She had pulled the supply wagon he'd ridden in and found a path that wouldn't jolt his tiny body out onto the road. Now she frolicked and grazed, brought out of his distant memory to pass on at least a little memory to Val's own children.

"I can see Flick!" Lusi, knelt on her bench with her hand hovering over the illusion of the piebald horse Val had had to retire only last year. "He looks so young!"

"He gets to be young again here." Val sent miniature Flick—as he was when he'd first got him—rearing up to almost touch his nose to Lusi's fingers, then dancing sideways through the flowers. He was rewarded by her laughter, and he smiled back. "I think he likes it too, don't you?" When the bards weren't claiming he rode the wind, they named Flick as his mount. They taught armies to yell *Cavallan rides*! and expect him to dramatically appear to save the day. Rose had taught him to laugh at the irony embedded in bard's tales, but there was always another summons and battle cry to deal with. He swallowed down his frustration and sent the horses cantering into formation to prance in wide circles. "Anything else?" He couldn't hold the landscapes forever, not against the endless power drain, but long enough for this.

"Can we put the horses in the hills now?" Lusi asked hopefully. "Please, Da!"

Emlan sat up, pulling his elbows clear of the table, and wrapped his arms around his knees instead. "Go on then. I had my turn…"

Val let the illusion fade, wiped away the plains map, and drew a new hills one in its place. He'd seen this one so often in recent years that he barely had to search for it. Another trickle of power and the hills rose out of the table: grass-sloped, tree-speckled, edged and capped with reddish-grey stone. He added the same herd of horses, grazing around a tree in the central valley.

Lusi beamed. "Riders too!" she begged. "I want to see riders on adventures with their horses!"

Val looked up and caught Rose's crooked smile across the room. Trust Lusi to want adventures… He exhaled slowly, just short of a sigh, and added a line of horses with riders, cresting the ridge above the herd's valley and sweeping down to join the other horses. There was Jake, with his permanent grin and prosthetic hand. There was Mak: friendly, graceful, welcoming, deadly. There was John, his armour glinting and surcoat flaring around him from the speed of his ride. Friends. Old friends. Lost friends, conjured from memories. Here he got to see them again, outside of dreams, and he watched them ride as eagerly as Lusi.

The horses took off as the riders drew close, and pounded away between trees and across a brook. Droplets of water sprayed up from their hooves to soak the chasing riders. Val kept his focus on the illusion and left Lusi's vigorous delight to haunt the corner of his vision. This was just riding, just a race. No battle waiting at the end of it, no danger along the way. The horses and riders swooped up a slope, over the peak, and down the other side into a clearing, then circled around and raced along the edges of the illusion: past Lusi, across the table, and back past Emlan.

The drain was beginning to tell on him. He could feel the exhaustion rising through his body like a thundercloud. Val brought all the horses back into the biggest valley, milled them around briefly, then lined them up so that they spelled out "Happy Birthday Emlan and Lusi!"

Lusi clapped. Emlan grinned. Val held the illusion a moment longer before letting it fade out. He wiped the table clean and leaned back in the chair while he recovered. "So," he said with a smile. "You enjoyed that?"

"Yes!"

"Spotting Flick was awesome! And he got to run and have fun and everything with all of the others!"

"I liked the brook, and all the water flying up around them!"

"All right, what next?"

Rose replied before anyone else could. "It may be your birthday, but you still have lessons to get to today. You didn't get out of archery practice and you don't get out of reading and sums, either. Come on, you can still show off your new cloak pins to your friends."

They brightened at that thought and scattered to collect their slates, bags, chalk, and cloaks.

Val put Lusi's chalk back in her pouch and tossed it to her. "I'll walk you down to the guilds again, if you like," he offered. "Then you'll have me for as long as possible."

Lusi fumbled the catch and had to scoop the pouch off the floor.

Emlan looked from Val to Rose. "Can't you both come?"

Rose smiled. "I don't see why not. Lessons are at the Weaver's guild today, anyway." She checked they had everything and herded the twins out of the door.

Val followed, and the twins came to flank him again: Lusi on his left, Emlan on his right. "How are your lessons coming along?" he asked, and that was apparently all it took to release a flood of chatter from Lusi.

She talked about the sums they did, and the sentences they read and wrote on slates, and how, if they did very well, they were going to advance to learning how to lay out money balances soon, and how their friends were doing. Emlan injected a phrase or two occasionally, but mostly it was Lusi, and all Val had to do was listen and nod at the right moments. Rose strolled behind the three of them, and Emlan turned to look back at her from time to time.

At last they reached the Weaver's guild. Emlan waved and elbowed Lusi. Lusi rolled her eyes at her brother and then waved as well, before vanishing through the doorway at a run.

Rose drew level with Val. "Well, now they are eight. What do you think?"

"You've done a good job of bringing them up," he told her, gazing after them. "I'm just glad to see them get this far."

"You do a fair job yourself," she reminded him. "When you're here."

"When I am, perhaps. But I'm not, often enough."

Rose laughed and shrugged. "You made it clear enough that you'd often be away when we drew up that contract of ours. It's nothing new."

Val grinned back, pulled his gaze away from the guild house, and started back down the road. "Thank you for figuring out a contract that worked—still works—for both of us."

Rose fell in beside him, but all she said was, "You're welcome."

A Gallant Rescue

A.P. Raymond

Robin climbed through the access tubes in the bowels of their ship, hand over hand, as they passed rebuilt sections, panels blasted with dents or scorch marks, and chunks of ladder slightly melted or completely replaced. The *Oure dere Lady* was an old ship—a patchwork of emergency repairs, scrounged replacements, and haphazard upgrades. All in all, it was a glowing testament to the skill of the engineers who loved her. The forward viewing chamber, once the aesthetic highlight of the ship, was a beautiful space meant to be utilized for crew recreation. Now, after several refits, it was only accessible via a hand-over-hand (or, in Scathlocke's case, tentacle over tentacle) climb through three decks' worth of access tubes. Essentially, it was wasted space, but Robin didn't mind. For the crew members who could get to it, it was a refuge. The chamber gave a breathtaking view of the endless black ahead of them, sprinkled with the bright pinpricks of stars as they danced in their orbits.

Robin flopped down on an old couch facing the viewports. Only their own soft breathing filled the room until a series of grunts filtered in from the access tube. Johnny slid onto the deck with a clumsy thump, her large frame never terribly agile when climbing through the bowels of the ship. Or ever, really. Robin raised an eyebrow at their second-in-command and partner, smirking as she staggered to her feet and dusted off her trousers. "Good trip?" they said with a devious grin.

"Har har, Rob." She picked up their feet and sat down at the other end of the couch, setting Rob's feet on her lap. "Message from your Granddad to not dawdle on the way back to port."

"We're already at top speed." Robin then sat up. Something in her voice had sent a chill down their spine. "What did he say?"

Johnny looked down at her lap and then out towards the stars, as if searching for Barnsdale Port off in the distance; as if she could will them closer. "Ellen's family is pushing her to marry an off-worlder, someone her father has business ties with. She's not sure how long until the pressure becomes an ultimatum."

They took a deep breath, centering themself. "How did Ally take that?"

"Scathlocke and Much are with her, but she's not doing well. We need a plan."

"Yes. Yes, a plan would be a *great* idea… Can she even get out of her family compound right now?"

Johnny shook her head. "No, she's not allowed to 'wander' anymore. She had to hack a comm just to contact your granddad." She sighed. "I remember the day Ally came back from busking with that ridiculous grin on her face, all aflutter."

"Young love. It's grand." Robin laughed.

Smiling warmly at them, Johnny said, "It sure is." And her grin stretched even further as Robin felt their cheeks grow warm. "Be better when Mattie's back."

Robin sighed. "No word yet? We might not be able to wait around port until Mattie shows this time."

"Your granddad is packing up the post."

"He's what?"

"Well. You know we're gonna go help Ellen run. No matter what, someone is gonna tie us to her disappearing. We won't be able to go back to the port for a long time, if ever. Your granddad said to make space for his stock in the cargo bay. He's joining us." Johnny took her partner's hand, rubbing her thumb over Robin's scarred knuckles. "This is going to change a lot. But I think it'll be good."

"As long as we can keep Ally from going off the deep end in the meantime," Robin said as they took a deep breath. "And if we can fit all granddad's stuff onboard."

Johnny barked a laugh.

Barnsdale Port was much like any other primarily Human-colonized settlement. Dirty, poverty-stricken, full of people with nowhere else to go who arrived—if lucky—with the clothes on their backs. Like a slick of oil on top of the ocean, a small group of wealthy business owners and bankers floated above the less fortunate, sucking credits from the rest of the population. The wide, sprawling shipyards spread out from the port itself. It was a constant urban decay piled higher and higher. The tallest towers reached towards a purple sky. Penthouses were built, filled with the luxuries of a dozen planets, while the lower levels descended to the poorest of the poor, who were actually on the ground. Climbing the social ladder had a very literal meaning here.

For centuries, Humans had reached toward the stars, and now the wealthiest could look out and touch them, even see Sol flicker in the distance from their wall-sized windows and their rooftop gardens. Yet always, the poorest were chained to the ground, grubbing for scraps.

The upper classes didn't even bother to touch the ground by going down stairs or elevators, preferring their hovercars if they wanted to touch planetside. The tall towers almost completely disconnected the social classes, with covered walkways and mid-air trams built for the workers, and dirt and old pavement at ground level. Meanwhile, the bright lights of the rich drowned out the stars. A haze of light pollution from their opulent towers kept everyone else from even dreaming of other planets, other places, other lives. Though Barnsdale Port was just over a mile square, it had grown even higher. The support pillars for the upper levels sometimes sank right through the poorest buildings in the city.

Johnny had grown up on the lowest levels, the original plasteel streets covered in layers of dirt mixed with things she didn't want to think about. Like most of the rest of her crew, she had worked in the various trades that would take a child's quick eyes and small hands until she had grown, and grown, and scrabbled enough money together for an estrogen implant, making herself into herself. On the other side of town, she had met Ottar, and eventually, the wily old man's grandchild, Robin.

Love came hard for people at Barnsdale Port. Meeting Robin had changed the course of Johnny's life; gave her a new family, and a new trade. Building on literal generations of work as a go-between for the dirt-scrubbers and the ever-squeezed middle class, Ottar scrimped together just barely enough money for a wreck of a ship. With a ship came freedom, if you could keep it. Keep it fueled, keep it running, keep it away from the scum that would steal it from under your barely cooled body. Decades of Ottar's work, and his mother's work before him, and her bibi's work before that, all on the hope of something more for Robin. They were the only child of their line to stick to the family instead of joining the Port Corps or signing on for passage off-planet at the first opportunity. Luck, cruel business deals, and seizing the first chance they got had all given Robin the chance to be the first in generations to set foot on another planet and then come back. With work done and more acquired, they had managed to run a slim enough profit to sock away for the bad months when work was thin. This was the crew, and the family Johnny had found. Robin and their childhood sweetheart, Mattie, welcomed Johnny as soon as they met. The little trio stumbled over one another for near an entire Terran year before their first kisses, to the never-ending amusement of the rest of the crew.

* * *

Mattie, always on the move around the system, found eir skills as a coder in demand if ey didn't ask too many questions about what ey was doing for the credits. Credits that paid for ship parts, or medicine, or a month's protection for Ottar from the gangs that roamed the lower levels of the port at the direction of upper crust bosses.

Ey moved from shadow to shadow along the dockyard's rutted streets. The small shacks lining each side were built by some of the poorest who breathed ship exhaust and burned in the heat of a too-close liftoff. But the *Oure dere Lady* sat somnolent at the end of the street, where Mattie would find eir lovers returned. Ey hoped. Slipping up the ship's gangplank, ey found the main cargo hold near empty, only a few crates strapped to one bulkhead. And there was Johnny, doing a cute little hop to settle the half a dozen weapons Mattie knew she kept at hand on any planet or station, even the one attached to a vague sense of home. Maybe especially then.

"Hey."

Johnny whipped around, grin broad and happy as she caught sight of her other partner. "Hey. Welcome back." She opened her arms and Mattie fell into her gratefully, head tucked under Johnny's chin.

"I should be saying that to you." Mattie let her hold eir tight. They stood together, swaying softly in the cargo hold, for several minutes. Pulling back, Mattie smiled up at her and lovingly traced eir hand across Johnny's cheek and the jagged scar that graced it. "You good?" Johnny nodded. "Robin?" She nodded again. Mattie breathed a sigh of relief. "Ally?"

Soft footfalls sounded from the passageway. "She's not doing well," Robin said, moving into Mattie and Johnny's joint embrace as Mattie gestured to them. The trio huddled together, breathing each other in.

"Mattie." A soft, weary voice broke through, the three of them pulling apart to look over at Ally. Her normal, bright-red busking clothes were absent. Instead, she wore all darker colors, mismatching pieces obviously filched from her crewmates' bunks, but perfect for blending in around the port. And instead of her electro-hurdy-gurdy hanging by her side, she wore a bandolier of stun blades across her chest. "It's good to see you." She offered a wan smile, and Mattie separated from eir partners to enfold Ally into a hug.

"Oh, Ally." In a moment, Mattie had Ally's full weight against eir, as Ally wept bitter tears. "We'll get her away. We will."

Ally soaked Mattie's shirt with her tears, and sniffed as her crying tapered off. "Ellen's been worried about it so long, Mattie, or something like this. Her father, the bastard, he wants the connections her marrying that creep would give him. The influx of cash for his business. And she kept saying she wanted to leave, but what would she *do*?"

Robin inched closer, resting their hand on Ally's shuddering back. "She'll come with us. You know she's always been welcome."

"*I* know that, but she… she wants to be *useful*. She didn't want to just run without a solid plan."

"She makes you *happy* and that's what matters. There's plenty she can do to help us, if she needs to," Robin murmured, rubbing soft circles on Ally's shoulder blades. "We'll figure something out once she's here. Right now we have to get her out."

As a group, they glanced out the open cargo hatch, which faced Barnsdale Port. The city's towers climbed to scrape at the sky, with levels and levels of life visible. The mid-range actual streets and walkways connected buildings; the mazes of ladders, streets, and walkways at the lowest levels climbed starward. All of it built up to the open spaces where the rich depended on hovercars. Even getting up to the levels where Ellen lived would be a challenge: only workers with official identification were allowed past the cadres of armed guards. Ellen herself had slipped through the security checkpoints on her first visit down to the middle levels where she saw Ally busking. She'd then barely made it back through to her own father's home after the system's twin suns set.

"He put a tracker on her. Like a criminal," Mattie growled, thinking of Ottar's pale face as he'd described his hurried conversation with Ally. "I talked to your granddad, got more info than that comm he sent you. She can't find her toolkit to get it off, and the servants are banned from even talking to her."

Ally sobbed, roughly wiping her face with her sleeve before she fingered a stun blade. "What do we do?"

Robin shifted uncertainly, Johnny shrugged, and Mattie bared eir teeth in a razor-sharp smirk. "Oh, I have a plan."

The sky was full of stars. In nearby space, a handful of manned stations and artificial satellites orbited the planet, blinking their ways across the dome of the world, providing an ever-growing array of man-made constellations. Three moons, all in different phases, offered a pitiful amount of light to the lowest levels of the city. Most of the crew of the *Oure dere Lady* moved through the abundant shadows, avoiding the streetlights and their attached security cameras, until they slipped through the back door to Ottar's trading post.

They reassembled, huddling loosely in the cramped room where Ottar both kept his meager back stock and slept. Only Scathlocke had abstained from the mission, as being one of the few of her species in Barnsdale made her stick out like a sore tentacle amongst the mostly-Human population. Scathlocke's absence meant that Robin, Mattie, Johnny, Much, Tucker, and Ally were crammed into the small space, dressed in dark clothes, each and every one heavily armed.

There was nothing to do but fidget while waiting. Robin sighed, gesturing for Johnny to sit before they pulled a long strip of dark green fabric from their pack. Deft fingers wove the fabric into Johnny's hair, using it to disguise her bright blue strands and hold it back from her face. They could all hear Ottar in the front of the shop, chatting with a customer, and stayed silent as the transaction completed. A few moments later, the door creaked open, and Ottar startled slightly to find his back room crowded with people instead of cargo containers. He zeroed in on Robin, his face lighting up.

"You, come here, kid," he said, smiling as he pulled his grandchild into a strong embrace. Robin sunk against him gratefully. Mattie and Johnny moved behind their partner, and as soon as Robin was released, Ottar hugged the pair of them, before offering a handshake and a smile to the others. He stopped in front of Ally, whose jaw was tensed like iron to avoid quivering. "Oh, honey." He drew her into his arms and let her sob twice before she regained control. "You don't worry. We'll get her free."

Ally shook her head. "You're giving up everything for us. How can we—"

"Shush. Never let it be said I stood in the way of love. And maybe I want to see more of the universe than just this port. Eighty years old and I've never left the ground. I think it's time for an adventure, wouldn't you say?"

"Yes, sir," Ally replied, her gaze dropping to her feet for a second, shy and blushing.

"And an adventure you'll get, Granddad. Are you packed?" Robin asked.

"About as well as I can and still look like I have stock up front. I can get that set in an hour, quicker with help." He straightened up, one hand on his cane.

"Well, best close down, and we'll get you packed. Scathlocke will be here with the grav-sled in an hour to get everything aboard and Tucker can stay to help."

A flurry of activity filled the trading post, and soon, the rest of Ottar's wares were packed up and stacked by the back door for Scathlocke to load. When the grav-sled rumbled up to Ottar's loading dock, Ottar went to greet her. The rest of the group double checked their weapons before slipping back into the shadows, heading toward the ground beneath where Ellen was sequestered by her family.

Robin stared up towards the highest levels of the city, which they'd shortly be invading. Ally shifted at their side, longing and fear writ across her face, her bottom lip between her teeth and her eyes wide. Behind them, Johnny and Much did last-minute checks of the climbing gear. "What if she doesn't want to come?" Ally moaned, tugging at her hair. "What life can I give her but crew on a trade ship? She's giving up…" She waved at the top of the tower ahead of them.

"She's giving up nothing she isn't willing to part with," Mattie said softly. "It's not a hard choice, when what she gains is so much more than she's leaving." With a smile, ey added. "Trust me, it's not a hard choice to make. Wasn't for me, won't be for her."

Ally turned, barely able to make out Mattie's expression in the dark where they all huddled below a broken security light.

Mattie laughed, and leaned against Robin. "I didn't fall from *quite* the social height Ellen is going to, but high enough. And it wasn't a choice I had to think about at all; my heart made it. I gained everything when I fell for these two."

Robin lifted up one of Mattie's hands and pressed a kiss to eir knuckles.

Johnny finished with the gear and twirled Mattie into her arms for a soft kiss before setting eir down with a gentle nose-boop. "As delightful as love is to talk about, it's even better to live it. Now, we've got a tower to scale and a fair maid to rescue from durance vile." She helped both of them slide into climbing harnesses and then spit at the crumbling durasteel building in front of them. It was a leftover from the original colonization of the port before the structure now hunched over it had been constructed. It supported a multilevel tower system that reached towards the stratosphere. "Onwards and upwards, folks."

An average walking pace for someone with two working legs was a mile in about twenty minutes. With their gear, going a mile into the sky took a full two hours. Each movement was meticulous and careful as they worked around crumbling edifices, security checkpoints, and buildings lit up by their inhabitants. Ellen's message, smuggled out to Ottar, gave exacting directions to where her family was holding her. By the time they were all sweating from exertion, and more than a little fear from having to constantly look down at the thin air below them, the group understood how necessary those directions were.

The buildings at the highest level of Barnsdale Port were smooth plasteel and transparent aluminum, and so far above the ground that most people eschewed balconies due to wind shear. Instead, the rich preferred the sheltered artificial parks and arboretums for outside activity. The only proof they were in the right place lay in a single, small sign Ellen left against the sealed-shut window.

"Right here," Johnny called downwards from lead position of the climbers. Robin moved up beside her and unslung the heavy construction laser from their back. In a few moments, it clamped securely to the window, and Ellen's face appeared a few feet to the side, her hand pressed hard and flat on the clear surface, mirrored outside by Ally's, tears running down both their cheeks.

"You two are adorable, but get her a little further from the laser, Ally. I don't want her so close to where we're cutting." Robin smiled, waving at Ellen.

It took half an hour to cut a person-sized hole in the window, and then carefully push it inside for Ellen to catch. Each of them climbed through, making five soft thuds on the impossibly-thick carpet before securing the room from the inside while Ally held Ellen close. She pressed kiss after kiss to Ellen's cheeks as Ellen smiled through her tears. Meanwhile, Much attacked the ankle tracker while maneuvering around the couple, pinching Ally to get her to move enough for xyr to have access. Cutting it off would set off dozens of alarms throughout the building, so reprogramming it was their best option until they were clear of the port. Much took xyr time prying the front panel off to avoid triggering the alarm, and then hooked it to a small independent coder's system. Connected, xe handed the entire mess over to Mattie, who couldn't splice two wires together but was a genius with programming.

The sun had just started to spill a soft glow over the horizon, cutting off the option of going back the way they came unnoticed, when Mattie smirked as the ankle tracker softly beeped twice. "We're good. For about three hours. Time to get the hell out of here."

Ellen, smiling too widely to speak, pointed at a pile of clothes in the corner.

"Yes, love?" Ally squeezed Ellen's hand.

Ellen found her voice. "We'd be noticed in a second climbing down, so I filched uniforms from the laundry before they were sent out." Her smile fell. "My father," she spat out, "in his generosity, gave me free rein of the household, if not the port or access to my things. I've made the most of it. Luckily, he has a rather large staff that is always rotating because no one can stand the slimy bastard. A few new faces won't raise too many eyebrows until after they notice I'm gone."

Johnny laughed as she slid on a security guard's helmet with a mirrored eye guard that covered the top half of her face. "What an idiot."

In ten minutes, the group was suitably attired in uniforms and helmets. Ellen led them, disguised as well, through the halls. She limped slightly, the tracking anklet jammed uncomfortably into her boot. The household slept as the group made their way through empty passageways, weapons in hand. The guard posted to the door lifted his hand as if to gesture that they stop, but before he could speak, he crumpled to the floor as one of Ally's stunblades slammed into his chest.

Robin glanced around. "Alarm on the door?"

"I don't know. I haven't been allowed to even touch a door in three months," she whispered back.

Much crept forward to study the access panel set in the middle of it, Mattie by xyr side. Before Much and Mattie could figure out how to open it, the door swung open, nearly slamming into Much. They both jumped back as Johnny surged forward to seize whoever was incoming and Mattie grabbed the door itself.

Cutting off the newcomer before they could call out, Johnny hauled him into the room and slammed him into the doorframe. He groaned, half unconscious from the force Johnny had used, whimpering slightly. Older, gray-haired, and dressed in the finest clothes to be bought anywhere in the system, the man was dazed. Johnny held him up.

Ellen's eyes widened, but she gritted her teeth and stepped forward to slap the older man across the face. "Goodbye, Father," she snarled as Ally handed her a stunblade. With a sharp smile, Ellen pressed it into his chest, the bolt firing into his chest and knocking him out.

"We have about thirty seconds before this door starts shrieking," Mattie whispered.

Johnny dragged the unconscious man inside and then waved everyone out. The door clicked behind them, giving them perhaps twenty minutes of lead time before the guard and Ellen's father awoke from the stunblades.

"Time to *move*," Robin hissed, and waved Ellen into the lead. In their security uniforms, even with their strange collection of gear, no one stopped the group as they jogged in a semblance of military formation through the nearly-empty halls of the building, heading towards the stairwells staff used to move between levels. They burst through the stair doors, Much whirling to secure the lock, just in case.

Much glanced down the deep stairwell, which was half-lit and poorly maintained. "I feel like I'm going to puke today."

"We're all probably going to puke today, Much." Robin laughed. "Let's get going. We have to get out of this level before anyone notices anything."

With Robin in the lead and Johnny at their back, the entire group started down the stairs. All of them were soon breathing hard, reaching out to steady anyone who tripped as they raced down the stairs. Twenty-two minutes after jamming the stairwell door, alarms shrieked. They reached the third floor of the highest level of the city, just three floors away from the security checkpoint they had hoped to slip through unnoticed in their uniforms. Instead, the pale blue light of the stairwell washed red under the alarms, and everyone drew their weapons.

"Halt!" demanded one of the guards at the checkpoint below them.

Mattie answered with a stun grenade tossed down the stairwell before ey pushed as many of eir crew as ey could reach towards the wall. The stun grenade exploded, the force of it shoving at their backs, and groans and pained cries came from below. Mattie started pushing them down the stairs once more, taking the lead from Robin. At the base of the stairs, sprawled across the floor in front of the security checkpoint, were half a dozen guards, unconscious or close enough.

Mattie frisked three of them before ey popped up with a keycard and grinned. "Got it."

After prying a panel off, Much plugged physically into the system and slid the card through the identlock. A few frantic keystrokes accompanied an audible click as the security door released.

"When do we get out of these uniforms? Mine keeps riding up my butt." Ally panted as they started a steady run through the mid-level of the city. As a group, they stood out, but in the uniforms, they were ignored as if part of the scenery. In the mid-level, with residents more dependent on ground transport instead of hovercars, there were wide, enclosed boulevards for walking and driving, and it was through these that they bolted. Colors and shapes were all a blur as they made their way through mostly unfamiliar streets. Ally led, using every shortcut learned during her illegal busking days to guide them through a near-warren of access roads and back alleys.

In the very back of a crumbling alley, Robin called a halt and started to strip out of their stolen uniform. Much, hauling the construction laser, set it up to bore through the cracked pavement. As alarms rang across the city's mid-level, the laser cut through the ground and the plasteel foundations holding up a third of the city. After a quick recheck of their climbing gear, and then securing Ellen into the spare harness, the group prepared to descend into the lowest levels of Barnsdale Port.

The hollow thud of debris hitting the building below alerted them that the laser had finished its job. Prying the tool back up, Robin secured the climbing ropes, then urged Johnny down first, letting her guide and call soft-voiced instructions up to Ellen, then Ally.

The entire group stood on the top of an apartment building. Before anyone could catch their breath, Johnny easily pried the roof door open, and they descended creaky, near-collapsing stairs to street level.

Still inside, prior to stepping outside, Robin switched on their comm, barking into it. "Situation!"

"Comm traffic tells me they haven't even found your climbing hole...yet, and think you're still mid-level. But going by standard protocol, we have about fifteen minutes before they lock down the port." Scathlocke's reply came through even though the comm was full of static. "Everything is loaded and we're prepped for departure. Tucker's strapped everything down in the hold."

Robin and Johnny glanced at one another. "Okay, let's split up. We can get through the streets unnoticed a lot easier if we're not one big group."

Much nodded, opening the door carefully to peer outside. Xe gave a thumbs up, ushering out Ally, already firmly holding Ellen's hand as the pair of young lovers darted into the early-morning crowds. Mattie drew Johnny down into a quick kiss before patting Robin's cheek and taking off with Much.

"Well, I see where we rate." Johnny laughed, dragging Robin behind her as they started to jog towards the ship. In the chaos of a Barnsdale morning commute, no one seemed to even notice them.

Sweaty, sucking in great heaving breaths, the pair was the third and last team to climb aboard. Robin slammed on the gangplank controls, wincing at the great screech of metal and plasteel that echoed through the airlock. "Go, go, go!" they screamed towards the bridge as soon as the gangplank secured, the airlock seals around it hissing loudly. With a great lurch, idling thrusters roared to life. Robin hung onto the console for dear life as the *Oure dere Lady* rose into the morning sky.

Hand over hand, they pulled themself along the corridors, Johnny right behind them. Stumbling onto the bridge, they flopped into the nearest empty seat and strapped in. Scathlocke sat at the helm, Ottar to the side monitoring the port's communications, and Much on the engine console. The ship was more than ready for escape velocity.

Robin glanced around and saw the rest of the group had all strapped in. Ellen's face was pale as she gripped Ally's hand. Tucker was keeping a close eye on the ship's systems while Mattie worried over last-minute flight plans. And Johnny surreptitiously powered up the weapons—just in case.

Robin breathed a soft sigh of relief. "That went well."

Mattie choked out a laugh. "Really? Really, Rob?"

"Well, all things considered. We managed." They waved a hand toward where Ellen was practically in Ally's lap, the two of them strapped into a bench seat for takeoff. They glanced at her ankle: the tracker gone, a bandage in its place. They frowned. "Not a perfect extraction, I suppose, but we got the job done."

"We're almost out of atmo, and definitely off the local scanners," Scathlocke noted, the slight hiss in her voice betraying anxiety. Robin looked out the front viewports, watching as the ship skimmed through the highest clouds halfway around the planet from Barnsdale Port.

"Take us out as soon as you have a clear shot, Scath," Robin ordered, slumping into the seat as their adrenaline started to crash. They rubbed their eyes and fought back a yawn.

"Aye, Robin." Scathlocke used her fourth tentacle to ease the ship into a jump, the stars blurring as they slipped around moons and asteroids and past the system's outer planets. The stars grew brighter, the solar light fading as they left behind the port's comm traffic.

Ottar breathed an awed sigh as they sped past the great gas giant at the very edge of the inner part of the system, its ice-covered rocky moons swarming in mining robots that blinked against the dark of space. "We're out of range," he murmured, before fully ignoring the comm panel to gaze out at his first glimpse of the stars. He gasped, one thin, leathery hand pressing to his chest as tears ran down his face. "It's *beautiful*."

Robin tried to look out at the familiar sight of space, space, and yet more space, with fresh eyes, like their grandfather who worked for decades to buy a spaceship and then never even left the ground. "It is." They unbuckled from their jump seat to move forward and set a hand on Ottar's shoulder. "You're going to see it all, too, I promise." They turned to wink at Ellen, a silent promise for her as well in their words. "The sky's the limit," Robin murmured, the old adage not quite accurate as Scathlocke slowed the ship down to navigate the first of three outer asteroid belts.

"Where to, Captain?" Scathlocke stretched her beak into her species' equivalent of a grin.

"Ellen and Granddad have spent all their lives on a desert rock," Robin mused. "Let's show them somewhere green."

"Sherwood Colony it is," Scathlocke commented, punching in the coordinates.

"That's near a month out from here," Ottar said.

"Plenty of time to plan a wedding," Johnny stated, then laughed as Ally turned beet-red. Ellen blushed more gently, lifting Ally's hand to press a kiss to her love's palm.

"More than sufficient," Robin said. "I think Ally and Ellen have waited quite long enough, and what we have arranged, let no man tear asunder." They ran a hand through Johnny's hair, mussing it as she made mock-outraged noises, before turning into her embrace. Mattie slipped eir arms around them both, content.

From her seat, Ellen nestled against her, Ally began to sing...

Come listen to me, gallants bold,
Of green and gold and life to hold
Of love and merriment and maidens fair
Lest anyone doubt the romance of the stars.

About Our Authors

Nyri Ani Bakkalian

Nyri A. Bakkalian is a queer Armenian-American and adopted Pittsburgher. A military historian by training, she's an artist and writer whose work has appeared on Inatri, Metropolis Japan, Gutsy Broads, and Queer PGH. She has a soft spot for local history and unknown stories, preferably uncovered during road trips with her girlfriend. When not hunting for unknown history, Nyri can most often be found sketching while enjoying a good cup of Turkish coffee.

CONNECT WITH NYRI:
Website: sparrowdreams.com | Twitter: @riversidewings
E-Mail: thesparrowsdream@gmail.com

Evelyn Deshane

Evelyn Deshane's creative and nonfiction work has appeared in Plenitude Magazine, Briarpatch Magazine, Strange Horizons, Lackington's, and Bitch Magazine, among other publications. Evelyn (pron. Eve-a-lyn) received an MA from Trent University and is currently completing a PhD at the University of Waterloo. Evelyn's most recent project #Trans is an edited collection about transgender and nonbinary identity online.

CONNECT WITH EVELYN:
Website: evedeshane.wordpress.com | Twitter: @evelyndeshane
E-Mail: evelyndeshane@gmail.com

Carolyn Gage

Carolyn Gage is a lesbian feminist playwright, performer, director, and activist. The author of nine books on lesbian theatre and seventy-five plays, musicals, and one-woman shows, she specializes in non-traditional roles for women, especially those reclaiming famous lesbians whose stories have been distorted or erased from history.

In 2014, she was one of the six featured playwrights at the 53rd *Annual World Theatre Day*, sponsored by UNESCO, and held in Rome. In 2014 she also received a *Lifetime Achievement Award* from Venus Theatre in Laurel, Maryland. Her collection of plays *The Second Coming of Joan of Arc* and *Selected Plays* won the *Lambda Literary Award in Drama*, the top LGBT book award in the US.

CONNECT WITH CAROLYN:
Website: www.carolyngage.com
E-Mail: carolyn@carolyngage.com

Shira Glassman

Shira Glassman is a bisexual Jewish violinist passionately inspired by German and French opera and Agatha Christie novels. Her best known works are the *Mangoverse*, a series of fluffy fantasy novels centering women that has made it to the finals multiple times in the *Bisexual Book Awards* and *Golden Crown Literary Society Awards*.

She lives in north central Florida, where the alligators are mostly harmless because they're too lazy to be bothered.

CONNECT WITH SHIRA:
Twitter: @ShiraGlassman

Sacha Lamb

Sacha Lamb is a part-time librarian, part-time goat-herder, and part-time writer of queer Jewish fiction for teens. As a teenager, Sacha loved YA fiction, but never felt represented in it as a gay, transgender reader. Now a graduate student in library science, Sacha is dedicated to creating stories for others who need to know they're not alone.

CONNECT WITH SACHA:
Twitter: @mosslamb
E-Mail: sivuster@gmail.com

A.P. Raymond

A.P. Raymond (they/he) is from Massachusetts (USA). A handful of identities resonate with them, including trans, nonbinary, queer, and bisexual. When not furiously scribbling down ideas, he enjoys nature photography, cooking, knitting, tending a forest of houseplants, and catering to the whims of the family cats.

CONNECT WITH A.P.:
Twitter: @apraymond3
E-Mail: darmok3@gmail.com

Kay C. Sulli

Kay C. Sulli is a queer asexual writer of historical fiction, historical fantasy, and lots of stories set in the woods. Not unlike any other errant tumbleweed she goes wherever the wind takes her. She journeys through the tales of shifters, vampires, and sometimes even humans. Never far from her trusty fountain pens she can often be found adventuring across the landscapes of the American West with a camera and a notepad to capture the stories all around her.

CONNECT WITH KAY C.:
Twitter: @kaycsulli
E-Mail: kaycsulli@gmail.com

E H Timms

After winning the BBC Wildlife Young Poet of the Year award, E H Timms eventually went on to write full time. She now has a children's novel and a poetry anthology published, as well as work in magazines, anthologies, and ezines from England to Australia. She lives in South West England with far too many books

CONNECT WITH E H:
E-Mail: ehtimms@btinternet.com

Teresa Theophano

Teresa Theophano is a New York City-based social worker and freelance writer. She is the co-editor, with Stephanie Schroeder, of *HEADCASE: LGBTQ Writers and Artists on Mental Health and Wellness*, forthcoming from Oxford University Press, and editor of *Queer Quotes* (Beacon Press, 2004). Teresa is also a former contributor to the now-defunct websites xoJane.com and glbtq.com.

She co-founded the NYC Queer Mental Health Initiative, a peer-based support organization, in 2014, and the LGBTQ Camaraderie Project, a nonprofit that develops prevention-based training curricula to encourage mutual aid among queer and trans community in the hostile sociopolitical environment, in 2017. Teresa is on the board of Trinity Place Shelter for LGBTQ homeless youth, and is currently at work on a full-length memoir as well as a co-written volume on suicide prevention and postvention in LGBTQ communities.

CONNECT WITH TERESA:
E-Mail: teresatheo@gmail.com

Other Books from Queer Pack

www.queer-pack.com

Reintegration

Eden S. French

ISBN: 978-3-95533-926-5
Length: 388 pages (139,000 words)

Streetwise cyborg Lexi Vale brokers deals for gang lords in the anarchic city of Foundation. Her mind-reading implant gives her a crucial edge—but now its creators want their tech back. To survive, Lexi seeks refuge with an eclectic group of rebels and outsiders. When she discovers an emotional connection amidst the chaos, she finds herself fleeing not only her hunters, but her oldest secrets.

Coming from Queer Pack

www.queer-pack.com

Queerly Loving

(Volume 2)

Edited by G Benson and Astrid Ohletz

Queer characters getting their happy endings abound in this first book of a two-part collection. Discover pages upon pages of compelling stories about aromantic warriors, trans sorceresses, and modern-day LGBTQA+ quirky characters. Friendship, platonic love, and poly triads are all celebrated.

Lose yourself in masterfully woven tales wrapped in fantasy and magic, delve into a story that brings the eighties back to life in vibrant color, get lost in space, and celebrate everything queer.

Get ready for your queer adventure.

Queerly Loving (Volume 1)
© 2017

Miss Me With That Gay Shit (Please Don't) © 2017 Sacha Lamb
Gifts of Spring © 2017 Shira Glassman
Wishing On The Perseid © 2017 Kay C. Sulli
Hunt and Peck © 2017 Teresa Theophano
First Light at Dawn © 2017 Nyri Bakkalian
Dragons Do Not © 2017 Evelyn Deshane
Planchette © 2017 Carolyn Gage
Birthday Landscapes © 2017 E H Timms
A Gallant Rescue © 2017 A.P. Raymond

ISBN: 978-3-95533-950-0

Also available as e-book.

Published by Queer Pack, legal entity of Ylva Verlag, e.Kfr.

Ylva Verlag, e.Kfr.
Owner: Astrid Ohletz
Am Kirschgarten 2
65830 Kriftel
Germany

www.queer-pack.com

First edition: 2017

Credits
Editors: G Benson and Astrid Ohletz
Coverdesigner: marceline2174.tumblr.com